DEAD MAN'S BRIDGE

ALSO AVAILABLE BY ROBERT J. MRAZEK

FICTION

The Bone Hunters

Valhalla

The Deadly Embrace

Unholy Fire

Stonewall's Gold

NONFICTION

To Kingdom Come

A Dawn Like Thunder:
The True Story of Torpedo Squadron Eight

DEAD MAN'S BRIDGE

A JAKE CANTRELL MYSTERY

Robert J. Mrazek

CROOKED
LANE

NEW YORK

Published in the United States by Crooked Lane Books, an imprint of The Quick Brown Fox & Company LLC.

Crooked Lane Books and its logo are trademarks of The Quick Brown Fox & Company LLC.

Library of Congress Catalog-in-Publication data available upon request.

ISBN (hardcover): 978-1-68331-269-7
ISBN (ePub): 978-1-68331-270-3
ISBN (ePDF): 978-1-68331-272-7

Cover design by Craig Polizzotto and Andy Ruggirello
Book design by Jennifer Canzone

Printed in the United States.

www.crookedlanebooks.com

Crooked Lane Books
34 West 27th St., 10th Floor
New York, NY 10001

First Edition: August 2017

10 9 8 7 6 5 4 3 2 1

To Jim and Ann with love

Every guilty person is his own hangman.

—Seneca the Younger

1

Her desolate moan dragged me back from the abyss. I could hear the spatter of hard rain against the cottage windows. A peal of thunder erupted above us as the storm slowly rolled east toward the Adirondacks.

She was trembling when I reached across the bed to stroke her back. As she labored to find a more comfortable position, she kicked me in the leg before falling back into a fitful sleep. The nightmares were coming more frequently now, and I wondered if the chemotherapy treatments were responsible.

Her oncologist had warned me that the chemo might cause serious side effects. But without the treatments, he said that the cancer would almost certainly metastasize. She had borne the injections with silent fortitude.

Her night breathing had become increasingly spasmodic. I remembered my awe at her physical agility and grace when she was young. It was hard to witness the toll the disease had taken on her energy and strength.

The first time I saw her was in a remote Afghan village beyond the Khyber Pass. It was early winter, and an old mujahideen had been about to disembowel her for his next meal. Back then, her thick coat had been pure white and she was as big as a calf. In spite of the indignity of being shackled to a rusty chain, there was a hint of royalty in her manner.

I asked the old man what kind of dog she was.

"Only Allah could be sure," he growled in Pashto while continuing to sharpen his knife. "I think . . . half wolf . . . half deer."

He might have been right. In quiet repose, her face was sweet and gentle, almost like a fawn's. When her blood was up, she had the primeval glare of a timber wolf about to ravage its prey.

I gave the old man a gold sovereign and kept the dog. A few nights later, I was in the mountains and waiting for orders on the next raid. A cloud of flying insects had descended on our camp. As I sat close to the fire, the dog began leaping into the air with incredible speed to capture them in her mouth. That's when I decided to call her Bug.

She was my closest companion for the next five months. Unlike a number of my human brethren, she was intelligent, loyal, and brave. On a frigid night near Kandahar, her growled warning had saved my life.

Another mournful sigh broke the stillness as lightning lit the sky. Through the window, I watched the bolt strike the earth on the other side of the lake. My father used to call it the finger of God.

I knew I wouldn't get back to sleep. Trying not to disturb her, I walked through the open French doors and out to the wraparound porch. Standing in the darkness, I inhaled the smell of wet moldering leaves. A few days of raw October wind had stripped them from the trees and left them a couple inches deep on the grass leading down to the lake.

I heard Bug drop from the bed to the floor, and she slowly came through the French doors. Her eyes were like two chocolate moons in the jagged white face, her rear legs quivering. In the years we had been together, her white coat had gone increasingly gray.

She had been as fast a dog as I have ever seen. Now she couldn't walk from the bedroom to the kitchen without panting. My veterinarian's best guess was that she was eighteen years old.

I went back to the kitchen and picked up the open bottle of Johnnie Walker on the counter. I emptied a couple of fingers into her water bowl. She lapped at it contentedly until her left hind leg began quivering again. Moving over to the rug by the fireplace, she flopped down onto her stomach and began licking her front paws.

I sat in the Morris chair on the porch and took a hit of scotch. There were three hours to kill until dawn. A shaft of moonlight emerged from the low silvery clouds.

The night air felt close. It reminded me of the hurricane seasons when I was stationed at Fort Benning in Georgia.

"Heavy weather on the way," I said to Bug while rubbing my knees. She looked up at me with her luminous chocolate eyes before flopping onto her side and letting out another low moan.

I considered my own bout with melancholy. The first psychiatrist the army had assigned me during my court-martial had concluded that I was depressed. No medical training was required to figure that out. I had killed eleven men in Afghanistan, and three of them were on my own special operations team. A night doesn't go by that they don't visit me, their mutilated dead faces in full Technicolor.

The psychiatrist assured me that my depression was pathological and that it could be cured with psychotropic drugs. He was a born-again Christian and strongly recommended that I also let his Savior into my life.

A second psychiatrist was assigned as part of the legal team defending me on the murder charges at my court-martial. She arrived at the same conclusion as the first one: I was depressed. Unlike the first shrink, she told me that depression was part of human nature, a gift to us ever since the Romans worshipped the god Saturn.

"Whenever you feel depressed, Major Cantrell," she said after our first session, "welcome Saturn into your heart . . . embrace him like an old friend."

I took another swallow of Johnnie Walker. After its fiery glow receded in my throat, I picked up a book from the stand next to the Morris chair. It was an old friend of mine, a pulp fifties paperback by John D. MacDonald. Between swigs, I tried to get through the first page.

I thought about the army-issue 1911 Colt .45 that was sitting in the hollowed niche next to the chimney. Over the years, the handgrips had been worn smooth. It would be so simple. A swift pressure of finger on trigger and the familiar whiff of cordite. Why not make my final count an even dozen?

The jarring ring of the landline telephone came through the open porch doors. I decided not to answer. It kept on ringing, and I made a mental note to put in a voice mail message if I was still around on Monday. After a dozen rings, I got angry. Whoever was calling had obviously decided to let it ring forever. I went into the living room and picked it up.

"Officer Cantrell?" came the timid voice. It sounded hoarse and urgent. "This is Carlene."

"I know," I said, recognizing her voice.

Carlene was one of the new provisional campus security officers and worked as a dispatcher on the midnight shift.

"You're needed here right away," she said.

"What time is it?"

"A little after five."

"My shift doesn't start until eight, Carlene."

"I know, but . . . this is an emergency."

Emergencies were rare at St. Andrews College. Our most recent one involved a female student majoring in pre-wed. After getting jilted by the captain of the hockey team, she had swallowed a handful of amphetamines and run amok at the Kappa Kappa Gamma sorority. I asked Carlene if the girl had escaped from the county hospital.

"That isn't funny," she said, her voice rising. "You're needed here right away."

Carlene always seemed to be on the verge of tears. I recalled one of the other officers telling me that she was undergoing grief counseling after breaking up with her own boyfriend.

"An individual just called in from one of the blue emergency boxes to report that we have a deceased male individual on the campus," she declared with the kind of quasi-official jargon mandated by Captain Janet Morgo, the chief of the campus security force.

Bug had followed me inside and was glaring at the phone as if she resented the intrusion as much as I did.

"It's probably a prank," I said.

"I don't think so," she replied, her voice getting shrill. "It was a man on the phone. He hung up before I could ask him anything else."

"Why not call Captain Morgo?" I came back, not wanting to drive into town after draining half a bottle of scotch.

That's when she blew.

"I hate this job!" she shouted into the phone. "Why am I always left here alone at night?"

"Calm down, Carlene," I said.

"Do you think I would be calling you if there was anyone else to handle this?" Carlene yelled. "Captain Morgo is on the road back from the conference in Albany, and I can't reach her on her cell phone. Lieutenant Ritterspaugh is having contractions, and Officer Hurd is on vacation in New Mexico. You're the fourth-ranking officer in the department."

Her tone suggested that the sacred trust had been left in the hands of the Boston Strangler.

"All right, sweetheart. Where is this body supposed to be?"

There was more exasperated breathing before she said, "The caller told me that the deceased individual was hanging from the suspension footbridge over the Fall Creek Gorge. In a few hours, it will be in plain sight of the alumni arriving for homecoming weekend."

"Call the sheriff's office," I advised.

"I can't do that," she objected. "After the last student incident on the bridge, Captain Morgo implemented a strict policy of campus police being the first responders."

In May, an Asian American honors student had committed suicide by jumping off that same bridge. It had ended up as a feature story in the *New York Times*. Bad for college recruitment.

"Call the sheriff's office, Carlene," I repeated in what I hoped was a reassuring voice. "I'm on my way."

2

I drove into Groton along the gravel road next to the lake. My old Chevy pickup rattled in mortal agony as I held it to fifty on the rough surface. Bypassing the town square, I headed up Campus Hill on the steep grade that bordered the Fall Creek Gorge.

Off to my right, a two-hundred-foot-high cataract of black water was cascading down the raw sandstone canyon. Thirty thousand years ago, a glacier had retreated through this part of upstate New York like a giant plow, carving out the bedrock and leaving deep gorges in its path.

This chasm separated the campus of St. Andrews College from the residential neighborhood that adjoined it. In the 1930s, President Roosevelt's WPA had constructed a suspension footbridge across the gorge to connect the two.

Rooming houses, fraternities, and sororities dotted the residential side. Most of the college kids living in the neighborhood used the footbridge as a shortcut to reach the academic quad. Unfortunately, the bridge had also become a magnet over the years for stressed-out students looking to put an end to more than their academic careers.

As I continued up the steep grade in first gear, the Fall Creek Tavern emerged out of the gloom. Called the Creeker by the locals, it clung to a shale plateau next to the road, the rear wall sagging out over the two-hundred-foot abyss. The Creeker's regular closing time was four AM. Through the open front door, I could see a barmaid sweeping the cracked linoleum floor.

Ben Massengale was standing under the side portico, smoking a cigarette and waiting for the place to reopen at six. He waved at me and smiled, exposing his dire need for advanced dentistry. I waved back.

The grassy overlook next to the footbridge had six parking spots. They were all occupied. The college enforced a one-hour time limit on the spaces, and I saw that all but one had been ticketed for an overnight parking violation. The unticketed car was a vintage Saab station wagon with a peeling bumper sticker that read, "Save the Arctic."

Dawn was paling the eastern sky as I parked my truck at a steep angle ten feet from the precipice of the gorge and next to the brick path that led to the bridge. Taking my police badge out of the glove compartment, I pinned it to the chest of my blue pullover. Grabbing a flashlight and a pair of clean cotton work gloves, I slid over to the passenger side and leaned hard against the badly sprung door.

I was almost through the opening when the wind whipped it back, and the door slammed into my kneecap. A jolt of pain raced up my right leg. Waiting for it to subside, I took a few moments to scan the bridge.

From end to end, the steel span was about fifty yards across. Its walkway was six feet wide and covered with poured concrete. Five-foot-high iron railings bordered each side. The space beneath the railings was covered with steel mesh to prevent an accidental fall.

I could see something slowly swaying in the darkness halfway across the bridge and directly underneath it. What might have been a body was hanging from a rope about ten feet beneath the walkway. My first thought was that it could be an elaborate hoax, a fraternity prank to welcome the alumni back for homecoming weekend.

Limping past the parked cars, I touched the hood of the unticketed Saab. It was cold, but I made a mental note of the license plate number. In the glare of the flashlight, I could see a raw gouge in the paint on the rear fender. It looked as if someone had scored the paint with the head of a screwdriver. The gouge extended around the side of the car. Training the flashlight beam on the adjacent car, I saw that its door panels had been scored the same way.

As I hobbled down the brick path to the bridge, I wondered why the county sheriff's office hadn't already dispatched a patrol car to the scene. They would have been there before me if Carlene had phoned them after I hung up. I decided to call in from the emergency phone at the entrance to the bridge.

The blue emergency light above the telephone was haloed in mist. Flipping open the door of the metal housing, I found a bare wire. Its copper ends had been cut. I remembered Carlene saying that the man had called from an emergency phone. This was the only one in the area.

An owl called out in the elm tree above me. Otherwise, the only sound was the rush of water down the gorge. The houses along the street were dark. I glanced over to the other side of the bridge. Nothing moved in my line of sight.

Putting on the work gloves, I paused at an engraved plaque that was bolted onto the stanchion at the entrance to the bridge. "This facility was painted through the generosity of Arnold Rhatigan, '73," it read. Similar plaques adorned the campus like chrome dandelions.

As I headed out across the bridge, I swept the walkway ahead of me with the flashlight. The surface was wet from rain. It was unmarred. Halfway across the span, I came upon a length of rope strapped around the left railing. It had been secured with a simple stopper hitch. The rope was an inch in diameter, and the end of it was braided into four different-colored strands. The tip was capped with what looked like a golden acorn. There was something vaguely familiar about it.

My eyes were drawn to several objects on the concrete walkway. A thin booklet lay against the foot of the railing beneath the rope. The cover was green and gold with black lettering that read, *Your St. Andrews Welcome Home Alumni Guide.*

Beneath the words was a color photograph of the footbridge I was standing on that had been shot in autumn sunshine with the maple trees ablaze in the background. Pinned to the booklet was a plastic name tag. "Dennis Wheatley" was written in black calligraphy. A green plastic reunion mug sat next to the booklet. There were a couple of inches of liquid remaining in it. I recognized the aroma of blended whiskey.

I leaned out over the five-foot-high railing. Two hundred feet below, the cataract of water tumbled down the rock-strewn gorge. About ten feet below me, the large object was swaying back and forth at the other end of the braided rope. The flashlight beam brought it into clear view.

It was no hoax. He was real.

The dead man was wearing a blue-and-white-striped seersucker suit with white penny loafers. One of them had apparently dropped off. He wasn't wearing socks. A green reunion baseball cap was still stuck on his head, the bill skewed to the side. Ringlets of grayish-blond hair spilled out below the lower edge. From the angle where I was standing, I couldn't see his face.

I moved another five feet along the railing and trained the beam on the man's face again. His grotesquely swollen eyes were staring vacantly across the gorge toward the campus bell tower. Like every dead man I've seen, his eyes reflected no light. The front of his shirt was crimson with blood.

I had never seen rope burns cause such a wound. Whatever had actually snared him around the neck was buried deep inside the skin and had apparently caused the profusion of blood.

The dawn light was bringing everything into focus, and I turned off the flashlight. As I moved away from the railing, I felt something dislodge from its surface and caught it in my left hand. It was a small slick of caked brown mud. There was a second clot about twelve inches farther along the top of the railing. Walking along the edge, I spotted three more.

"I'll take over from here, Officer Cantrell," came a deep voice from the residential side of the bridge.

I turned back to see Captain Janet Morgo coming toward me. Ken Macready, a new provisional security officer, was right behind her. Beyond Macready, I saw Captain Morgo's SUV parked in the middle of the street. She hadn't activated the strobe lights on the roof rack.

Captain Morgo was dressed in the uniform she had personally designed for the campus security force after she had been appointed to the job. The blouse and pants were a matching burgundy with a thin band of gold piping down the pants' seams and gold thread stitched around the pockets. The hat had enough scrambled eggs on the brim to satisfy a French admiral. Someone in the office told me it had won a fashion award at the national campus security officer's convention.

Her Glock 17 pistol was holstered on the belt that rested on her hips, along with several leather pouches holding her flashlight, cell phone, and stun gun. There was nothing soft or feminine about her. She was six feet tall, husky, and powerful. I had seen her bench-press three hundred pounds in the campus gym.

Before taking over the campus force, Captain Morgo had been in charge of the county juvenile detention home. When it came to management style, she took no prisoners. It was as if she thought that being feminine in any way would undercut her authority.

"Another suicide," she stated matter-of-factly.

I shook my head.

"I think it's a crime scene, Captain. We'll know more when the sheriff's investigative unit arrives."

I heard a screen door slam in the distance and looked back toward the residential side of the bridge. A few people were coming out of one of the houses, apparently drawn by the police car parked in the middle of the street. Word would now travel fast. Captain Morgo turned back to face me.

"I told Carlene not to call them," she said, the burgundy material of her uniform straining across her chest. "This is homecoming weekend. It's obvious we have another jumper here. As soon as we recover the body, I'll notify the Groton Police Department and then the county coroner. He can verify it. Now let's get him up."

"I believe this man could have been murdered," I said.

"So you say," she said, glancing back at the growing crowd of onlookers massing at the edge of the bridge. "He's the second jumper this year. We don't need to hold up a billboard to the world about these things."

I got the picture. In other words, our benevolent alumni would be less likely to open their checkbooks if confronted by the scene of one of their brethren hanging from the same bridge that was on the cover of the reunion booklets.

"We should bring in the sheriff's crime unit on this," I said without trying to sound confrontational. "This man is not an emotionally troubled student, and I've found several signs that point to someone else being involved in his death."

She sniffed the air between us like a point setter.

"Have you been drinking, Officer Cantrell?" she demanded.

I pointed down at the reunion cup at our feet.

"I smelled it too."

A small swarm of rubberneckers was approaching the bridge from the neighboring houses. Their voices rose as the first arrivals pointed out the still-swaying body to the rest of them.

"We can sort all this out later. Let's bring him up now," she said, leaning over to get a better view of the body. "Officer Macready and I will untie the rope and pull him up to the railing. Then I'll hold the line while the two of you lift him over the edge."

"I'd like to get another rope from my truck and get it around his body," I said. "The man's neck—"

"I'm in charge here, Officer Cantrell," she interrupted me. "You've heard my orders. Now let's roll."

As she loosened the stopper hitch, the rope slid down a few inches before she wrapped her powerful hands around it and heaved upward. Ken Macready stepped up to help her, and they began raising the body in a smooth hand-over-hand technique.

Bent over the railing, I watched the corpse rise upward. As was often the case in the moment of death, his sphincter had let go, and the smell wafted toward me as the swinging body drew near the edge of the steel underpinning.

"Stop," I called out as his shoulder lodged under one of the girders.

"What the hell are you doing?" demanded Captain Morgo, her face flushed with exertion. "Let's get him up here."

I could see that the snare was tightening around his neck under the additional drag. The man's head suddenly canted over to the left at an unnatural angle.

"Loosen the rope," I said.

The thick braided cord jerked down a foot or so, and his pinned shoulder came loose from under the girder.

"He's free," I said.

The swaying body rose toward my outstretched hands. I was reaching down to grab his right shoulder when I heard a loud squishy pop. It sounded like a soldier's boot being extracted from molasses-thick mud. A moment later, the man's head separated from his body.

A loud collective gasp came from the people at the overlook as his body began its long plunge to the bottom of the gorge. It landed spread-eagled on a massive flat rock in the middle of the torrent.

Incredibly, the man's head remained suspended in the air a few feet below the bridge, the garroted stub of his spinal column still rooted within the wire snare that had severed his neck.

"Mother of God," groaned Ken Macready when he looked over the edge. He crumpled in a heap on the footpath.

The crowd fell silent as the man's head continued to sway slowly back and forth at the end of the wire, his reunion cap tightly clamped over the grayish-blonde hair. Using my left hand, I gently pulled on the rope to bring him toward me.

He was an inch or two from my outstretched fingers when the head toppled free from the snare. Someone at the overlook let out a cry. A few seconds later, his head splashed into the roiling water below us. It bobbed to the surface for a moment as the cataract of water carried it along the rock-strewn canyon.

Captain Morgo was standing motionless beside me, peering down at the man's head as it disappeared over the first waterfall. I glanced at her hip to see whether she was carrying her VHF radio along with the rest of her tools. She wasn't. I began sprinting toward her squad car.

A bald man in pajamas was filming the scene from the edge of the overlook to the bridge. Plucking the camcorder out of his hands, I headed straight for the cruiser. Opening the driver's-side door, I grabbed the VHF radio from the charging unit on the communications console and punched in the emergency frequency monitored by the county sheriff's office and the Groton Police Department.

"This is Jake Cantrell, St. Andrews campus police," I said, keeping my voice steady. "We have a five-niner at the suspension footbridge over the Fall Creek Gorge. It's a possible code two. Send an investigative team immediately."

The sheriff's dispatcher immediately confirmed the request. I told the Groton police dispatcher to have the fire department send its rescue crew to the base of the falls in order to try to intercept the victim's head before it was carried into the lake.

There was a pause before I heard the dispatcher say, "Roger . . . will instruct."

I could only imagine their joint reaction to that piece of news. Outside the captain's SUV cruiser, the bald man whose camcorder I had grabbed was pounding on the window and demanding that I give it back to him. Swinging open the door, I stepped out, still holding the camera in my hand. Seeing me towering over him, he took a step backward.

"You can pick the camera up at the campus security office after we have examined the recording," I said. "Thank you for being a good citizen."

In the distance, I could hear the repeated echo of emergency sirens as I passed through the crowd.

"I think that's Jake Cantrell," said a man in the crowd.

"Jesus, it *is* him . . . it's the Tank," came back a second man.

The two male alumni were about my age. Both were wearing green-and-white St. Andrews replica football jerseys. One of them looked about six months pregnant. The other was clutching a bottle of Guinness in his right hand.

"Wish you were starting at fullback today, Jake," he called out as I moved through the crush. Ken Macready was standing guard at the entrance to the bridge. His young freckled face looked queasy. Two thin strings of vomit pasted one of his shoes.

"Sorry, Jake," he said.

"Don't worry about it," I said, giving his shoulder a tap. "The sheriff's crime unit ought to be here any minute. In the meantime, I think you should seal off the bridge at both ends with crime tape and get all the license plate numbers on those cars in the overlook lot. One of the owners might have seen something last night, and they should be interviewed as soon as possible."

"Yes, sir," he said.

"The emergency phone under the blue light at the edge of the gorge is missing. Whoever did this might have thrown it down there. It's worth a search in case there are prints."

"Yes, sir," he repeated.

I was still holding the camcorder.

"Take this back to the office when you're finished. It probably doesn't have anything worthwhile on it, but at least we won't be looking at a video of that man's head on the Internet."

As Ken started walking toward the police cruiser, I called him back. "Before you do anything else, use the camera to film everyone standing around the overlook."

"Yes, sir," he repeated again.

Captain Morgo hadn't moved from the spot where the man's body had been hanging. She stood there with her hands on her hips, glowering at me as if I were responsible for losing his body.

The end section of braided rope was still hanging over the railing. Lashed to it was a foot-long length of galvanized wire, the bloody loop tightened to a diameter of less than an inch.

It was concertina, the razor-sharp stuff we had used to protect our base camps in Afghanistan. Just a few weeks earlier, I had seen a roll of it being uncoiled around a local construction site after some local environmentalists had sabotaged one of their bulldozers.

"He was probably partying near here," I said to Captain Morgo, securing the rope and removing my work gloves. "My guess would be one of the fraternities over there. He looked the type."

"I'm well aware of your brilliance as a leader of men," she said, continuing to glare at me as two sheriff's cruisers raced to a stop behind the captain's SUV. A rescue vehicle from the Groton Fire Department arrived right behind them. The hulking figure of Sheriff Jim Dickey emerged from the second car and began striding toward the bridge.

"You are relieved," said Captain Morgo, as if she was George Patton and I had just failed to take Sicily.

I was limping away when she called out, "You aren't in proper uniform, Officer Cantrell."

I was still wearing the blue pullover I had slept in, along with jeans and sneakers. I considered telling her what I thought of her uniform but then thought better of it. After only six months on this job, my personnel folder was already filled with petty infractions. This one would probably dock another ten dollars off my monthly paycheck.

"You will report to me in proper uniform at oh nine hundred and be ready for a full inspection."

I passed Sheriff Dickey as he was coming across the bridge.

"Hey . . . it's the Soldier," he called out to me with a contemptuous grin as we walked past each other. Muscled like a steer, Dickey was my height of six two, but at least two hundred and eighty pounds, with gray crew-cut hair and a lantern jaw. About fifty, he had been county sheriff for almost twenty years.

"You kill any of your own men this morning?" he asked.

I ignored him.

"'Course it's still early yet," came his gravelly voice from behind me.

I glanced up at the morning sky. It had turned from ash gray to a bird's-egg blue. The big oaks and maples bordering the gorge seemed to take fire in the glow of the brilliant sun.

As I reached my pickup, a bright-red motorcycle came rumbling up the grade and pulled in at the overlook. It was an old Indian Scout, a classic that someone had lovingly restored.

The young woman riding it used her right foot to drop the kickstand after she braked to a stop. There was a police scanner mounted on the machine, and I could hear the chirping voice of a police dispatcher. In one smooth motion, she was off the motorcycle and headed toward the footbridge.

I stepped into the path ahead of her and held up my hand. She glanced up at the police badge on my pullover.

"This is a restricted area," I said.

"I'm Lauren Kenniston of the *Journal*."

In her late twenties, she was maybe five nine with a slim, athletic figure. She was wearing exactly what I was wearing, a pullover and jeans, but with riding boots instead of sneakers. She had probably been asleep when the call came over the scanner.

"That's great, but we're investigating a death on the bridge," I said. "No one is allowed out there right now except law enforcement."

"According to the report I monitored on my home scanner, it involves a headless corpse."

I was played out, or I would have kept my mouth shut.

"You'll need to talk to Ichabod Crane about that," I said. "Just don't come any closer."

Her big green eyes flashed with anger under a coronet of auburn hair.

"I have every right to cover a story affecting our readers," she said. "Let me talk to your superior."

She looked past me toward the bridge and called out, "Sheriff Dickey?"

I turned and saw Big Jim heading back toward us.

"Is this loser bothering you?" he called out as he came up.

"He is refusing to let me go down to the bridge."

"He has as much authority here as a warm bucket of spit. This is the famous Jake Cantrell. You probably read about what he did in Afghanistan. We had officers like him in 'Nam, and they usually got fragged. You should do a story on him."

"I'll sure think about it," she said.

"You come along with me," he said, putting his arm around her shoulder and leading her down toward the bridge. "It's all over though. Looks like another jumper."

She briefly glanced back at me as he led her down the path.

3

As I watched from the cab of my pickup, the Groton Fire and Rescue Squad unpacked its emergency gear, and two men prepared to rappel down the wall of the gorge to reach the dead man's body.

Captain Morgo was still standing in the middle section of the bridge next to Jim Dickey. She had lit her corncob pipe and was pointing authoritatively down toward the lower falls. The reporter was standing alongside them.

When I turned around, I noticed a green Volvo parked along the other side of the road. I knew the car. It belonged to Jordan Langford, the president of St. Andrews College, and the man who had gotten me the job on the campus force.

I found it odd that Jordan could have already heard about the man's death. Carlene would never have called him at home, and I was sure Captain Morgo would not have done so until she had personally checked out the scene.

Jordan emerged from the car and stood gazing out at the activity in the middle of the bridge for almost a minute, his mocha skin contrasting dramatically with the white tennis shirt and shorts he was wearing. I expected him to go down to the bridge, but instead he pulled a cell phone from his pocket and punched in a number. He said a few words into it, then got back in his car and drove away.

As I headed back down the steep grade, Ken Macready was standing unobtrusively in the shadows under the trees and filming the crowd of onlookers with the confiscated camcorder. He was going to be a good officer.

Farther down Campus Hill, the Fall Creek Tavern was open and already doing a thriving business. Through the windows, I could see more than a dozen men and women sitting at the bar in preparation for their daily challenge of remaining upright on their stools for most of the day. I was tempted to stop for a confidence builder but decided to go home and clean up for the captain's inspection.

Groton Lake lay tranquil as I pulled into the hard-packed gravel driveway behind my cottage. It was an old one-story cabin constructed with hand-hewn logs. There was a big stone fireplace in the pine-paneled living room. The primitive bathroom featured a claw-footed white enamel tub.

Bug greeted me at the door with a single wag of her bushy tail. I went to the refrigerator and removed the pot of garlic-flavored chicken I had prepared the previous evening. After heating a portion in a saucepan, I softened two cups of her favorite kibble with the broth and served it to her on the screened porch.

For almost a minute, she stared down at the chicken as if it were laced with strychnine. Then she began gazing across the expanse of Groton Lake as if contemplating a swim.

"Come on, baby," I said.

It was getting almost impossible to coax her to eat. Sometimes she went a day or two without consuming anything but water, and I would be reduced to pleading with her. As I was now. I selected a small slice of chicken out of her bowl and chewed it with gusto.

"Damn it, you eat better than I do," I said.

She looked up at me balefully with those big chocolate eyes, as if she was missing her home in the Khyber Pass and wondering why I had brought her halfway around the world to this godforsaken place.

"Julia Child slaved over this for you," I said.

After using the line so many times over the years, I didn't have the heart to tell Bug that she was dead. It rarely worked anyway.

"Cut the bullshit and eat it," I demanded.

As if granting me a royal dispensation, she slowly lowered her nose to the edge of the bowl and took an exploratory nibble.

"That's it. That's it," I encouraged as she chewed the first bite without enthusiasm.

She paused again as if waiting to be congratulated.

"Congratulations," I said.

She ate two more mouthfuls of chicken before pausing to lap up a few swallows of water. The bones of her lower rib cage were now protruding through the skin above her stomach. If things continued this way, the only solution would be to force-feed her, which I hated to contemplate any more than the idea of someone force-feeding me. Stepping away from the bowl, she trudged over to the daybed in the far corner of the porch and dropped onto her favorite quilt.

I had slept maybe three hours the previous night. In two hours, I was facing an idiotic inspection. Going back into the kitchen, I began brewing strong coffee in my blue enamel pot.

While it was heating, I walked down to the boathouse at the edge of the lake. I picked up the cracked leather gloves on the workbench and went over to the sand-filled canvas heavy bag that hung over the finger dock.

I began delivering shots to it, slowly at first, measuring the range.

Why had I come back here? I asked myself for the thousandth time. I knew it wasn't to endure the taunts of people like Jim Dickey, although I had heard plenty of worse things said about me during my court-martial trial. After I let the army finish me off, I didn't really care what happened anymore.

The heavy bag began to swing back and forth in an easy rhythm.

Part of the reason for coming back was that this place had been as close to a home as I ever had. I was twelve when my parents died together in a plane crash. My aunt and uncle sent me off to boarding school. I was pretty much on my own after that. At St. Andrews, everything had come together for me. Life seemed filled with golden promise.

And then I met Blair.

In truth, I had come back here because of her.

I met her during the fall semester of my sophomore year. She had come up from Wellesley for a football weekend, and she was at a party at our fraternity house the Saturday night after the homecoming game. From the first moment, I thought she was the most fabulous girl I had ever seen.

It wasn't just her violet eyes and wholesome beauty. She was animated and funny and projected an amazing blend of innocence and sensuality. We spent the rest of that night talking together in my room. I never touched her. Mostly we talked about literature, music, politics, and her dreams of helping change the world—"a world where children didn't have to grow up in fear of violence or hunger." She actually used to talk like that. I was convinced that if we had a lifetime together, we would never be talked out.

We spent spring break together camping in the Adirondacks. During the course of those few days, she awakened emotions in me I never knew I had. She made love with an almost savage passion. I felt such pride knowing she had become mine.

The next semester she transferred to St. Andrews, and we lived together our last two years in college. After graduation, we spent two months in Europe on a used BMW police motorcycle I bought in Amsterdam. On many of those nights, we would just pull off the road into a wood stand, wolf down the food we had bought at a charcuterie, and curl up together in our double sleeping bag.

I was inducted into the army when we got back, and she took an advertising job in New York. We spent my first leaves together. When I was deployed to Afghanistan, her gift to me was a silver dog tag. Engraved on it were the words, "To Jake . . . From Your Constant Heart."

Nine months into my tour, the letter came. She had fallen in love with another man, she wrote. She never meant to hurt me, it went on. It just happened. After that, the natural order of my life was gone.

Get over it, I had said to myself. Grieving over a lost love in this demented world was ridiculous. You've just managed to survive the mother of all battles. Move on. But I still loved her. I felt as if I had been cheated out of all the things that lay ahead of us.

I began whaling harder on the heavy bag, delivering pounding blows that I felt straight up my shoulder. At the end of another five minutes, the sweat was pouring off me, my knuckles were sore, and my arms were spent.

Stripping off my sweaty clothes, I went off the dock in a flat dive. I swam out into deep water, rolled over on my back, and floated for several minutes, looking up at the cobalt-blue sky.

I still carried the torch.

Swimming slowly back to shore, I picked up my clothes and walked naked up to the cabin. After checking to see that Bug was still asleep, I poured my first cup of coffee and shaved at the kitchen sink. I no longer used a mirror.

Whenever I looked in one, it wasn't with cool appraisal. It was an angry confrontation. "You stupid asshole" was my favorite personal greeting to myself. In the reflection of the windowpane, I saw the hazy image of uncombed hair and a blunt, wind-burned face.

The summer cottages on both sides of my cabin had been locked and shuttered for the winter. The woods were silent. From somewhere down the lake, I could smell burning leaves in the cool fall air.

When I turned on the radio, I was expecting to hear a news bulletin about the death of the man in the gorge. Instead, the news announcer reported that Hurricane Ilse had finished pounding South Carolina with 120-mile-an-hour winds. It was on its way north on a route that would take it up along the Alleghenies and possibly hit upstate New York early Sunday morning.

I found myself excited at the prospect. Storms have always wound me up. Mostly, it was the pure clean force of them—the blizzards, gales, hurricanes, even the one monsoon I had lived through.

After a shower, I found my least-wrinkled uniform in the closet and brushed the grayish-white dog hair off the burgundy blouse and pants. After a quick spit-polish of the dress shoes, it took me less than five minutes to press the uniform. That was another talent I had gotten very good at in the army. That and killing people.

Before leaving the cabin, I refilled Bug's water bowl and propped open the porch screen door with a paving brick so she would have access to the small stretch of grass that led down to the lake. She loved the freedom of roaming her tiny domain. There was no chance of her taking off. Unlike Blair, she would wait for me forever.

By the time I got back to campus, it was about eight thirty, and the roads into the college were swollen with newly arriving alumni. Traffic slowed to a standstill as they stopped in the middle of the streets to read the plastic signs erected to help them find their reunion classes.

They were of every age and hue, the older ones wearing straw hats and blazers. Most had name tags around their necks as they revisited the places where they had spent four years of their lives so long ago.

Some of the older alumni were already wilting and had stopped under the branches of the big oak trees that rimmed the quad. The current students surged around them, heading to the new campus learning centers.

Back when I had gone to St. Andrews, the quad had served as home to the arts and sciences. That's where we took all our courses. The buildings were the ivy-covered stone edifices with medieval arches that you still see in the recruiting guide.

Now those buildings housed professor's offices and support staff. All the classes were taught in the new campus learning centers. There was a Latino learning center, an Africana learning center, a nanoscience learning center, a computer science learning center, and an Asian learning center. A gay, lesbian, bisexual, and transgender learning center was under construction next to the campus store.

The college had undergone many changes in the century and a half since its founding. It was named by an early Scottish benefactor to the school after the original St. Andrews in Scotland, which is the third-oldest college in the English-speaking world.

With all the car traffic clogging the campus, I couldn't find a parking place and finally pulled into the lot behind the administration building, slipping into the last open space.

A painted sign on the curb read, "Reserved for Provost." Getting out of the truck, I placed my own cardboard sign behind the windshield wiper. It read, "Official Police Business." Putting on my uniform hat, I headed toward the campus security building.

A massive banner was stretched across the stone portals leading to the arts quadrangle. It read, "The Age of the Mastodon." There was a realistic rendering of a great woolly mammoth below it. He gazed down at me with a look of sad detachment, as if all he wanted to do was disappear back into his glacier. I knew exactly how he felt.

The campus police department was housed in a two-story brick building next to the student athletic facility. A few years earlier, contractors had ripped out the old plaster walls along with the crown moldings, wainscoting, and polished walnut doors. The new walls were about as thick as cardboard and the doors made of laminated plastic.

When I came in through the rear entrance, two kids were sitting on the oak bench inside the wire mesh holding pen at the back of the squad room. The first one looked like the Pillsbury Doughboy with curly red hair and pasty-white skin. He was crying. The other kid looked Spanish or Italian, with shoulder-length black hair and small, close-set eyes.

They were maybe eleven years old, both wearing baggy jeans shoved down below their hips, new basketball sneakers, NBA jerseys, and baseball caps cocked to the right side.

"You dog these hoes, man," said the black-haired boy. "It's you yo'self."

I figured them to be sons of St. Andrews professors in full rebellion.

"So what did you nefarious characters do?" I asked the red-haired one.

"We . . . uh," he began, wiping away tears. "We . . . uh . . ."

"Shut the fuck up, Cody," said the black-haired one.

"*Mi casa es su casa*," I said.

"You tryin' ta do me, asshole?" he demanded.

I headed across the squad room to my plastic-walled cubicle in the corner. I had just sat down at my desk when Carlene came in and headed straight for the coffee server against the far wall. She kept glancing at me out of the corner of her eye.

"Working overtime?" I asked, trying to make peace after our earlier conversation.

Ignoring me, she poured herself a cup of decaf, added three spoons of sugar, and left the same way she had come.

The rear entrance door swung open, and a stout man wearing an orange polo shirt and orange golf pants came into the squad room. After giving a fleeting glance to the boys in the holding pen, he walked over to me.

"Officer Cantrell," he said, looking down at my nameplate. "I don't believe I know you."

He was in his sixties with bloodshot eyes and a puffy nose. Red liver spots covered his bare arms.

"I'm sorry, but this area is off-limits to the public," I said. "The public entrance is at the front of the building."

"I'm not the public," he said. "I'm Roger Marcham. Why don't you just trot up to Janet Morgo's office and tell her that I'm here to see my clients."

He obviously thought the name would mean something to me.

"Why not just call Federal Express?" I asked. "They'll overnight you up there."

The black-haired kid in the holding pen snickered loudly.

"I will make sure your obnoxious behavior is conveyed to Captain Morgo," said Roger Marcham before he headed down the corridor.

The squad room phone began to ring.

"Cantrell," I answered.

"This is Jim Dill down at Groton Fire and Rescue," said the voice. "On that five-niner . . . we've had a team down in the lower falls for the last two hours."

"Did you find his head?" I asked.

"Negative . . . but we did find his hat."

"That's a start."

"We've got a diver in position at the entrance to the lake," he added. "A team of volunteers is going to make a search of the shallows at the base of the falls in about an hour."

"What's the prize for the lucky searcher?"

"Losing his breakfast," he replied.

"Thanks for the update."

My head was throbbing, and I went over to the small refreshment bar. I filled my mug from the coffeepot on the Formica table and went back to my cubicle to read the morning newspaper.

The lead story was about the Tenth Mountain Division being deployed overseas again out of Fort Drum. Remembering how well they had done in Afghanistan brought back a flood of memories. I turned to the sports section.

The cover page was devoted to the homecoming football game. Kickoff was at two o'clock. Coach York was expecting great things from his sophomore tailback. I put down the paper and yawned.

In the army, I had learned how to sleep just about anywhere and perfected a technique that allowed me to pretend I was listening to a bullshit briefing while keeping my head down, seemingly focused on the folder in my lap. The hardest thing to do was keep my head from nodding. I could go five or ten minutes in the same position and awake refreshed.

Pulling out a security office training manual from the shelf against the wall, I spread it open on my desk. Positioning one hand next to the page, I dropped my head over it. A few moments later, I was asleep.

"Officer Cantrell?"

I opened my eyes and looked up to see Lieutenant Ritters-paugh standing at the side of my desk and staring down at the training manual. She was at least eight months pregnant. Her maternity dress had red lambs knitted onto the white cotton background.

"Good morning," I said. "I was just brushing up on this manual about positive alternatives to incarceration."

"Yes, I can see that," she replied with a quizzical smile. "But I've been standing here for a full minute, and you never moved a muscle."

"The material is quite compelling," I said.

"May I see you in my office, please?" she asked.

"Of course."

I followed her down the hall and up the stairs to her office. As we walked along, I remembered a moment when I was marched to the principal's office after committing some infraction in the seventh grade.

Her office was at the end of the second-floor corridor. Its walls were painted a bright tangerine. A set of plastic shelves held houseplants in terra-cotta bowls. A stick of aromatic incense was burning in a miniature Buddhist shrine on her desk.

The digital clock on the wall clicked over to 8:59.

"Before we get started, I want you to know that I'm sched-uled for a full inspection with Captain Morgo at nine o'clock," I said.

"That has been postponed," she said.

Lieutenant Ritterspaugh was blonde, pretty, and soft spoken. I remembered that prior to joining the department, she had been a psychiatric social worker at the Groton Medical Center.

"May I call you Jake?" she asked.

I knew I was in trouble. One of the things we were taught in Ranger training was the interrogation technique that involved building intimacy with your captured prisoner before dropping the hammer on him. It was probably the same thing with former social workers.

"Sure," I said.

"Feel free to call me Emily."

"Thank you."

"I think you have the makings of a good officer, Jake," she began.

I remembered a light colonel in Afghanistan saying precisely the same words to me a million years ago. He was killed in the mountain caves at Tora Bora.

"I also believe we should go through life with openness to internal growth."

She paused as if waiting for me to say something. I didn't.

"You should know that Carlene was in tears when I arrived here this morning," she said next. "She is very intimidated by you."

"I have never tried to intimidate her," I said.

"Perhaps it's your aura," said Lieutenant Ritterspaugh.

"My aura?"

"We all have an aura, Jake. You happen to project a very strong one. Sometimes one's aura can cause unintended consequences."

"I would be happy to apologize to her if you think it would help," I said.

"I'm afraid it goes deeper than that. Carlene told me that when she called to ask for your help, you were flippant and dismissive and initially refused to respond to her request to come to the scene of the suicide."

So they had already concluded that it was suicide. I thought about confiding to her the reasons it was important to reopen the investigation. She didn't give me a chance.

"Carlene found your words personally insulting and deeply misogynistic," she added. "And if what she said is true, I have to agree with her."

"I never said anything misogynistic," I replied, trying to remember what I said.

"Do you remember making fun of the poor sorority girl who overdosed on drugs last month? Do you remember calling Carlene sweetheart?" she asked.

"Carlene was upset about being left alone. If I did call her sweetheart, it was just to calm her down."

"The call was recorded, Jake. The facts will speak for themselves when I review the recording. Have you ever considered awareness therapy?"

"What kind of therapy?" I said, keeping my voice calm.

"Therapy that could bring you into contact with your inner self," she said.

I was about to tell her that I would rather have a colonoscopy from Roto-Rooter when there was a knock on the door, and one of the secretaries poked her head in.

"I'm sorry to disturb you, Lieutenant, but Mrs. Wheatley is here, and Captain Morgo would like you to join them in her office."

She immediately stood up. "Well, Jake . . . we'll continue this conversation as soon as I return. It shouldn't be long."

I was sitting there wondering how I was going to keep my job when it struck me that Wheatley was the name that had been hand-written on the name tag pinned to the reunion booklet I found on the bridge. There was something else about the name, but I couldn't place it.

Wandering over to the window, I stared down at the campus. Two coeds were stretched out on the lawn below the police building. One was sunbathing and the other was tossing French fries to a couple of squirrels. Leaves from the majestic oaks were gently drifting down onto the freshly mown grass.

A woman's voice suddenly cried out in agony from beyond the open doorway. It had come from Captain Morgo's office. The anguished cry subsided to a low sobbing wail. Edging closer to the open doorway, I could hear Lieutenant Ritterspaugh's voice as she gently soothed the distraught woman.

"I'm so deeply sorry, Mrs. Wheatley," she said.

Leaning around the corner, I had a narrow view of the office through the crack in the door. A woman was standing in the center of the room, her delicate angular face wearing the stunned look of someone who has just been told she has an incurable disease.

Beyond her, Captain Morgo was sitting behind her desk staring down at the pager display of her cell phone. A man from the sheriff's plainclothes investigative unit was standing along the far wall making notes in a spiral notebook. Lieutenant Ritterspaugh had her back to me.

"Dennis would never take his own life," said Mrs. Wheatley, stifling another sob. "He had too much to live for. And he hated high places. He had a morbid fear of them. He would never have walked out on that bridge . . . much less looked over the railing."

In her midforties, she was no more than five feet tall with long black hair and a slender build. She had obviously dressed for a day of informal alumni parties, with a navy cotton blouse, white blazer, and pleated skirt over walking shoes. Her straw hat had a red ribbon around the crown. A white plastic name tag hung around her neck with block letters that read, "Evelyn."

"We have a preliminary laboratory analysis from the sheriff's office that indicates your husband had a very high blood-alcohol level, Mrs. Wheatley," said Captain Morgo.

"My husband didn't drink alcohol. Never. He hated it," she replied, her right hand slashing angrily at the tears on her cheeks and knocking the straw hat off her head.

"I will not cry," said the tiny woman fiercely as she picked up her hat.

"His blood alcohol-level would have been nearly twice the legal limit if he had been driving," Captain Morgo went on, "and there was a mug of whiskey near the spot where he died."

"And I'm telling you that Dennis didn't drink alcohol," said his widow emphatically.

"When something like this happens, it is always a terrible shock, particularly to close family members," said Lieutenant Ritterspaugh. "All too often, they are the last to know about a loved one's . . ."

"For God's sake," said Mrs. Wheatley, her quavering voice growing stronger. "This is my husband you're talking about. I knew him better than anyone in the world. And I'm telling you, he would never do such a thing . . . please . . . I would like to see him now."

The sheriff's investigator detached himself from the wall.

"I don't think that's a very good idea," he said.

Not when you haven't found the poor bastard's head, I privately agreed. At that moment, Carlene came around the corner and stopped short, startled to see me blocking the doorway. The momentary alarm in her eyes was quickly replaced by a look of triumphant satisfaction.

"The president would like to see you right away," she said. "His secretary said it was very important."

I was still straining to hear what the sheriff's investigator was saying to Mrs. Wheatley and whispered, "The president of what?"

41

"President Jordan Langford . . . the president of this college," she said with an exultant gleam.

Looking down at her, I realized that she thought the summons could mean only one thing. For all my transgressions, I was about to be cut off at the knees by the big kahuna himself.

"Thank you, Carlene. I'll check my calendar," I whispered.

Her liquid eyes regained their familiar confusion as she retreated down the hallway.

"Mrs. Wheatley," Lieutenant Ritterspaugh was saying through the partially open door, "I've had experience in working with victims of tragedy, and we have three very gifted grief counselors on staff here at the college. I would like to suggest that one of them might—"

"I don't need your goddamn grief counselors," shouted Evelyn Wheatley, her eyes flaring with anger. "My husband is dead, and I want to know why."

If I hadn't been hung over and fed up with my job, I would never have gone in there. Without stopping to think about the consequences, I pushed open the door and stepped inside.

Captain Morgo looked up at me and growled, "What do you want?"

"Mrs. Wheatley, did your husband ever serve in the military?" I asked.

"This is a private meeting, Officer Cantrell," said Captain Morgo. "Leave my office at once."

"No, he didn't," said Mrs. Wheatley. "Why do you ask?"

"That will be all, Officer Cantrell," ordered Captain Morgo, standing up and walking around her desk toward me.

"I don't believe your husband took his own life," I said. "He definitely wasn't alone out there on that bridge."

Captain Morgo planted her powerful body in front of mine.

"You are suspended from duty, Officer Cantrell," she said. "Now get out of my office."

I glanced over at Mrs. Wheatley. She was staring at me in my idiotic uniform as if I had just arrived from Mars.

I didn't salute Captain Morgo when I left. I heard the door close behind me as I went down the corridor. At the edge of the first open doorway, my eye caught a flash of color. A glance in that direction revealed the face of the auburn-haired reporter I had met on the bridge. She was staring back at me as if she had been caught shoplifting.

She had to have heard everything that had gone on in Captain Morgo's office.

I kept on going.

4

Walking across the sun-dappled quadrangle to Jordan Langford's office, I mused over the probability that I would soon find myself dropping to the next rung down the career ladder and tending the bar at the Fall Creek Tavern.

Ahead of me on the brick walkway, a student was tossing a Frisbee to an Irish setter. The dog leaped into the air to catch it on the fly, clamped it firmly in his mouth, and ran off past the statue of Francis Channing Barlow, the Union Civil War general.

Jordan's office was on the top floor of Hastings Hall, a granite edifice with medieval parapets and stone gargoyles perched at each corner. His suite took up the entire floor and had an impressive view of both the campus and the lake beyond. I could almost see my cabin from the reception area.

A young woman looked up from the receptionist's desk after I came through the outer plate-glass door. She was obviously a student intern. A two-inch-wide purple streak ran down the middle of her blonde hair, which was cropped at the neck as if someone had cut it with hedge clippers. An open paperback copy of *The Fountainhead* sat on the desk in front of her.

Removing my uniform hat, I said, "I'm here to see the Emperor of St. Andrews if he happens to be in residence at the moment."

She grinned, revealing two levels of metal braces. Over her shoulder, I saw Jordan come through the door of his office, his eyes absorbed in the folder he was carrying. Dropping it on his secretary's desk, he looked up and saw me.

"Do you know who you look like?" asked the intern, holding the eraser of her yellow pencil to her chin.

I shook my head.

"My favorite actor."

"Who is that?"

"Harrison Ford. Before he got old."

"I'm his illegitimate son," I said.

"Are you funning me?" she asked, her eyes widening.

"Jake," called out Jordan Langford from across the suite.

I followed him through the door and shut it behind me. Under the twelve-foot-high ceilings, his walnut partners' desk gleamed in front of the leaded casement windows. An oil painting of Benjamin Franklin dominated the wall above the fireplace. It hadn't been there the last time I visited.

"Your truck was illegally parked in the provost's personal space," he said. "She had you towed away."

"That's why you called me up here?" I asked.

He stared at me for several seconds.

"You look so ridiculous in that uniform," he said.

"Thanks."

He was dressed in a charcoal-gray, double-breasted suit with a white shirt and red-speckled power tie. Behind him, a power wall of photographs included pictures of Jordan with Bush the younger, Clinton, Obama, Mandela, and Beyoncé. I had met two of those same presidents. One of them had even pinned a medal on me. In looks and presence, Jordan was more charismatic than both of them.

"I understand you were the first one on the scene at the bridge this morning," he said.

"Yeah, aside from whoever it was that helped him over the railing. What were you doing there?"

I could see the question made him uncomfortable. I had known him since we were college roommates and knew how he reacted to just about any situation. He stared hard at me as if weighing whether to tell me the truth.

"Let's just say I happened to be driving by," he said.

"At six in the morning in your tennis whites?"

"Leave it alone, Jake."

I decided to leave it alone.

"Janet Morgo says you don't think Dennis Wheatley's death was a suicide."

"That's right."

It finally struck me who Dennis Wheatley was, or at least had been. Although I hadn't recognized his grossly contorted features when he was hanging under the bridge, he was the man who had become famous after creating a franchised chain of fast food restaurants designed to reverse America's trend toward obesity. He was the poster boy alumnus for St. Andrews College.

"We're trying to keep a tight lid on things for the moment," Jordan said. "You can probably understand why."

"Yeah," I nodded.

I remembered Dennis Wheatley from the series of funny, self-deprecating television commercials in which he offered Americans free bonus meals if they lost weight.

He had installed computerized cheat-proof scales that worked like ATMs in each of his restaurants so that customers could record their ongoing weight loss wherever they were. He was a multibillionaire and on the *Forbes* list of twenty richest Americans.

"There's something else," said Jordan. "Dennis Wheatley was a dying man, and he was increasingly despondent in recent weeks. I talked to him almost every day. He had pancreatic cancer, and it had metastasized. He told me the doctors only gave him a few weeks to live, and he hadn't told his wife."

"Why not?" I asked.

"Until a few weeks ago, he thought he had licked it," said Jordan. "It was in remission and then came roaring back. Evelyn Wheatley is . . . intense. He didn't want her to worry."

"She's on the warpath now."

"Evelyn also doesn't know that Dennis gave the college a gift of fifty million dollars two weeks ago. I was going to make the announcement at the trustees meeting on Monday."

"Who else knows about the gift?"

"Aside from Wheatley's portfolio manager, no one to my knowledge. Unlike most of the major pledges we receive, Dennis's gift was unrestricted. No strings attached. He just said, 'Jordan, do some good with it.'"

"You've already received it?"

"The money's sitting in my private discretionary fund account right now."

"What do you plan to do with it?"

"A global warming research center in his name," he said.

There was a knock at the door, and his secretary's face appeared around the edge.

"Congressman Cornwell is on the phone again for you from Washington."

"Tell Sam I'll have to call him back," he said with an easy smile as he sat down on one of the leather sofas. "I need ten minutes undisturbed, Jenny."

"Certainly," she said, closing the door behind her.

His smile disappeared.

I dropped my uniform hat on the other couch and sat down opposite him. Even though we were the same age, he definitely looked younger. His mocha-toned skin was as smooth and unlined as the day I had met him in college. At six feet, he was still lean and hard. There was a touch of gray at the temples of his close-trimmed black hair.

"I haven't seen you for a while. How's it going over there?" he asked, his expressive brown eyes locking onto mine.

"I have nothing to do," I said. "I do that well."

"You once did a lot of things well."

"Yeah . . . but I handed in my cape a long time ago."

"To say you're overqualified for the campus police would be a joke."

He was right.

"Look, I'm grateful for the job, Jordan. My prospects were limited. It was this or repossessing used cars."

"Janet Morgo wants you out of her department," he declared. "She told me last week that you're a bad influence on the rest of her team. She asked that I find you another soft landing . . . maybe the catering office."

"I was thinking about quitting anyway," I said, deciding not to bring up my suspension.

"To do what?" he asked skeptically.

"I'm thinking of running against Congressman Cornwell," I said. "There's a real groundswell of support out there. I'm already feeling it over at the Fall Creek Tavern."

Chuckling, he said, "I can handle Janet for now. She can be difficult sometimes, but she's a lot better than the last chief we had, believe me. You never met him, but he was as big a Neanderthal as Jim Dickey."

"That's hard to believe."

"So what else is new?" he asked, as if he had all the time in the world. It was obvious he wanted or needed something. I had no idea what it could be.

"A couple of guys think I should be starting at fullback in today's game," I said.

"If the Tank is ready to go, then so am I," he said with a grin.

Jordan and I had been the tandem backs on the only St. Andrews football team to ever win a Division III national championship. He had the footwork of Emmitt Smith and ran like a deer. I ran straight ahead like Riggins and carried the pile. He went all-American and was voted most valuable player. I had my left knee replaced.

"So let's cut to the chase. What do you need, Jordan?"

He stood and went to the open window that looked out over the quadrangle. I waited for him to tell me what was on his mind. I assumed it had something to do with Dennis Wheatley's death. Maybe all that money.

"I'm sure you remember that there was actually a time when I was deeply committed to the advancement of the human condition, Jake," he said as if dictating a term paper. There was another pause. He seemed to be waiting for my confirmation. I didn't say anything.

"Thanks to the inspiration of Dr. King, Medgar Evers, and a whole lot of others who blazed the trail, I've had the chance to explore those boundaries . . . through a legacy forged in blood. I've always treasured that. When I got back from the Peace Corps, I decided to work in the inner city in order to advance that legacy. I was a good community advocate. I really was," he said. "I earned my stripes during those years in Detroit just like you did in the army."

"Yeah, I know," I said, still wondering where it was all heading.

"And as I look back on it, I was happy then," he went on. "And Blair was happy." He paused again and said, "I think she was happy."

Blair was his wife. He was the one she left me for. After I had received her Dear John letter, I received a long one from him. Without apologizing, he tried to explain how it all happened. He hoped I would understand and forgive them.

"Anyway, she says she was happy. Happiness, peace, contentment . . . that's what life is supposed to be about, right Jake?"

"Sure," I replied. "You're talking to Mr. Happy."

I had never heard him sound so confused and bewildered. The Jordan Langford I knew had always been certain of everything, particularly his own blazing star in the universe. A lot of people had predicted he would be a senator or governor, if not president someday. I had always assumed that was one of the reasons Blair married him.

"We have a lot more of everything right now, but we're not content, Jake," he said, still staring out at the campus. "Blair and I argue all the time. She wanted me to stay in community work. I saw the chance to do a lot more on the executive side. I learned I had a talent for it . . . the gift of working with people and discovering that they usually came to believe in me . . . and to follow me. There are a lot of community advocates in this country, but there are very few good executives to marshal all that talent and make it work. I saw that when I moved over to the administrative side . . . that I could be exponentially more influential than as one good community organizer. It's all about the validity of how a man chooses to spend his life."

It was starting to sound like the beginning of a resignation speech. I wondered if he was thinking about quitting his job. Maybe he wanted to run for something. But he wouldn't have called me in to talk about that.

"You can take the position that everything has its validity on some level," he said. "I wasn't fearful of idealism back in Detroit. But many of the groundbreaking things I took pride in then somehow ring false today."

"Like what?" I asked.

"All right . . . take our minority faculty members. When you and I were here as students, this college didn't have any. Now thanks to me, there are more than two dozen . . . and they all claim to celebrate racial and ethnic diversity. But when I issued a directive last year that all incoming freshmen would have their roommates randomly selected so each kid could experience true diversity, they organized campus protests. I was branded an Uncle Tom and a lot worse."

"Yeah, I remember," I said.

"And it wasn't enough for them to have African and Latino learning centers," he went on. "Now we're building separate and segregated living centers."

He started pacing in front of the fireplace.

"Meanwhile I've got a government department full of professors who openly advocate the overthrow of capitalism while demanding six-figure salaries and threatening to move to other schools if they don't get a new pay package."

"Let them quit," I said.

His head shook back and forth.

"You don't understand what I have to deal with. Flaubert got it right when he said he tried to live in an ivory tower but a tide of shit kept eating away at the walls."

"I've got more important things to do," I said, standing up.

"Like what?"

"Like taking my dog for her chemotherapy treatment," I said. "Anyway, Captain Morgo suspended me from duty twenty minutes ago."

"Goddamn it. Now I'll have to kiss her ass to reinstate you."

"I really don't care, Jordan," I said.

"I put myself on the line for you after the army kicked you out."

I was almost at the door when he called out, "Jake . . . Wait!"

When I turned around, he seemed to be on the verge of losing his composure again. For a moment, I thought I saw actual terror in his eyes. Then the confident mask was back in place.

"I only meant that . . . look . . . I know you got a raw deal in Afghanistan."

"So long, Jordan."

I was going through the door when his final words stopped me in my tracks.

"I need your help, man," he said.

"What is it?" I asked, closing the door again.

"I'm being blackmailed, Jake."

5

"**I** was hoping you could help me find out who's doing it and get them to stop."

"So what have you done to be blackmailed?" I asked.

He pointed up at the oil painting of Benjamin Franklin and said, "No more than him."

In the painting, Franklin was wearing wire-framed octagonal eyeglasses and looked down at us from above the mantelpiece like a benign grandfather with a Mona Lisa smile.

"That's great. You're having an affair with Ben Franklin."

He gave me a wry grin and asked, "What do you really know about him?"

"Come on, Jordan. This is ridiculous," I said.

"Benjamin Franklin. What do you know about him?" he persisted.

"His face is on the hundred dollar bill. I wish I had a few more of them."

"What else?"

"He wrote Poor Richard's Almanac. And he had a big hand in drafting the Constitution."

"He also discovered the Atlantic Gulf Stream. And electricity."

"Yeah . . . it was all in the Disney movie."

"Right. Well Disney didn't include any scenes of Old Ben screwing his favorite prostitutes when he was seventy-nine years old . . . or mention that his diary was full of entries about his favorite sex toys and his fear of contracting venereal disease."

"I think I'm getting the picture," I said.

"Does anyone blame Benjamin Franklin for his little eccentricities? No . . . all they remember is that he was one of the greatest men of his generation or any other generation . . . but he was a randy old rogue."

"I assume there is a point to all this."

"The man was obsessed with women until the day he died . . . and I know just what was going through his mind. And now I'm going to pay for it."

"If you're being blackmailed, Jordan, then go to the sheriff or the district attorney," I advised. "They have people trained and equipped to deal with blackmailers."

"I should go and lay my problem at the feet of Big Jim Dickey? My career here would be over."

I wondered whether he had confided the problem to Blair and whether she had told him to ask for my help.

"You once said that part of your work in the army was coun-terintelligence, undercover work . . . secret surveillance and all that," he said.

"That's ancient history."

"I'm just asking you to try. You could at least try, couldn't you?"

Walking over to his polished desk, he unlocked one of the drawers with a key. Removing a brown envelope, he handed it to me. "There's a video recording in there. I'm the star. I'd like you to take a look at it in my study."

He pointed to a pocket door in the paneling against the far wall.

"You want to watch it with me?"

"Once was enough," he said as I headed for the door. "I'm afraid you're going to be pretty shocked."

"That would take a lot."

"Jake . . . you're the only one I can trust with this."

I nodded. The study was barely larger than a walk-in closet, but it was clearly Jordan's touchstone to a more idealistic past. Fastened to the back of the door was an old black-and-white poster from the 1960s showing policemen spraying black pro-testers with fire hoses in Selma, Alabama.

A scarred gray metal desk sat between the two walls. I remembered one like it from his first office in Detroit. Above the desk was a photograph of him as a boy in Mississippi and another of him and Blair shortly before they were married. The last one was with Michelle Obama.

A small television connected to a disc player sat next to a leather club chair. I removed the case from the envelope. It could have been purchased in any convenience store. The plastic cover was unlabeled. I turned on the television and inserted the disc.

It was a silent movie. The images were slightly distorted, as if the camera had been set too close to the subjects in the room. It had not been filmed with professional surveillance equipment. The picture was out of focus, although clear enough to identify Jordan. He was standing beside a woman next to a bed in what appeared to be a motel room. She looked Eurasian, with a slender figure and a delicate face.

The camera never moved. Its wide lens covered a queen-sized bed in the middle of the room and some of the area next to it. For the next twenty minutes, I watched Jordan and the young woman interact with each other. There was nothing remotely arousing to me about any of it.

After slowly removing the woman's clothes, Jordan picked up what looked like a small nickel-plated vibrator from a leather briefcase next to the bed and proceeded to give her a full body massage. He was very patient, starting at the soles of her feet and moving slowly up the legs, then up to her neck, shoulders, and back. The girl seemed to enjoy it, particularly when he finally brought the vibrator within range of her pubis. At the end she appeared to experience a deep orgasm. The disc went blank as she was putting her clothes back on.

He had been absolutely right. The encounter was deeply shocking to me, the reason apparent from the moment he first appeared on camera. Jordan Langford, the virile young president of St. Andrews College, former all-American football player, and the husband of my lost love, was dressed in women's lingerie—a lace bra and panties, with matching garter belt, silk stockings, and black high heels. An expensive shoulder-length black wig framed his face. His eyes were heavily accented with mascara and eye shadow, and he was wearing bold red lipstick.

When I came back out of the study he was standing at the window, still looking down at his college domain.

"You're right," I said. "I was shocked."

"I happen to dig exotic girls," he said as if that were the principal problem. "There's a service I use out of Syracuse."

"That wasn't it," I said.

"I know," he said, struggling to maintain his composure as I stared at him.

"Did you film it yourself?" I asked, knowing that some people liked to keep a record of their sexual adventures.

He shook his head and said, "I have no idea who filmed it. It arrived in the mail."

He handed me the brown envelope. It was addressed to Alicia Verlaine at a Syracuse post office box. There was no return address. It had been postmarked two days earlier from New York City.

"Well that's a start," I said, pointing to the postmark. "It narrows your suspects in the state down to around twelve million people."

His eyes hardened for a moment, but he didn't say anything. I took another look at the envelope. It had been slit with a letter opener. A single sheet of white paper lay inside, folded into thirds.

"You opened this yourself?" I asked.

He nodded and said, "Yes. Thank God."

I pulled out the small magnifier I kept in my breast pocket and examined the handwriting on the address. It was crudely written, as if the person had used his or her nonwriting hand to scrawl the words.

"It came to a special post office box I have," said Jordan. "When I order things . . . it's under an assumed name."

"I take it you're Alicia Verlaine."

He winced before finally nodding at me.

"The blackmail note is inside," he said. "I received it yesterday."

I unfolded the page. The lines were in red ink and matched the writing on the envelope. At first glance, the individual letters looked as if they had been scrawled by someone recovering from a serious stroke. They were scraggly and disjointed:

Alicia, if you want to avoid the public disgrace that will accompany the release of this sordid episode, you will give us five million dollars, payable under the instructions you will find in this envelope. Failure to do so by Sunday at five o'clock will result in copies of

it being distributed to all the national news
organizations.

"It sounds so goddamn matter of fact," he said, his eyes per-
plexed. "Like a dunning notice from a collection agency."

"Why tomorrow at five?" I asked.

"I haven't the slightest idea."

"It's the day before you're supposed to announce Wheatley's gift," I said. "It's entirely possible his death and the blackmail scheme are connected. Find the answer to one and it may
answer both."

"There's so little time," said Jordan.

"Has anyone attempted to contact you since you received the
recording?"

He shook his head and said, "I have no idea what's coming
next. The instructions provided me with an account number to
transfer the money to in the Cayman Islands."

"They may have no more plans to contact you if you decide
to pay them," I said. "Direct contact raises the risk of the blackmailer being caught."

"I don't have five million dollars."

"You have fifty million."

"That isn't mine."

"The blackmailer appears to know you have fifty. If so, I'm
surprised they aren't asking for more."

"I will not use his money. If you can't stop whoever is doing
this, I will resign at the trustees meeting."

I let it lie.

"Look Jordan, you never even screwed these women," I said. "There is no victim here, and it's clearly an act between two consenting adults. Hell . . . we live in the People's Republic of Groton. They celebrate the month of Gaypril here. There are probably more pagan ministers and UFO worshippers in this town than Baptists. It's as liberated a place as you could find in the whole country. No one cares what you do in your bedroom or your barn."

Shaking his head morosely, he said, "Don't you understand, Jake? This will wreck my career. It will make me a laughing-stock. And it will destroy my marriage to Blair."

I nodded.

"I take it Blair doesn't cut it for you anymore," I said with an edge of bitterness in my voice.

My tone obviously registered with him. His eyes seemed to fill with something like regret. Of course, he might have just been feeling sorry for himself.

"Blair is the best thing that happened in my life . . . she always has been, Jake. You probably won't understand this . . . but this thing, these liaisons . . . weren't about sexual release."

"No?"

"It was the . . . the adventure of it . . . the excitement . . . a macabre kind of dangerous theater . . . and the chance to give someone pleasure."

He was right. I didn't understand. He must have seen it in my eyes.

"It's true. I loved the thrill of it . . . and the danger."

"Why, Jordan?"

"I've thought about that," he said with a ghastly smile. "Maybe it's because I grew up the only boy in a family with a very strong mother and five sisters. Who the hell knows? It's not something I've brought up with my therapist."

"Maybe you should have."

"It's too late now."

"Not necessarily," I said. "Does Blair know?"

"God no. And that's the most important thing. I don't want to hurt her. I'll resign before I let her know."

"She may find out anyway."

"It would ruin us," he said.

I imagined her watching the recording and nodded in agreement.

"Yeah," I said. "And you're right about something else. The media vultures would have a field day with this story. All-American football star turned college president and future senate candidate prefers silk lingerie. In the day or two before they got a new target in their sights, you would be the poster boy on every tabloid television news show around the clock."

He visibly shuddered.

"Will you help me?"

"What about the woman you were filmed with?" I asked. "Could she be part of the blackmail plot?"

Shaking his head, he said, "She's an innocent kid . . . from Bali, I think, and barely speaks English. I've only been with her twice. None of these girls I meet ever know when I plan to call the service. I call the number and they send whichever girl is available."

"What about the service?"

"I've never actually been there. It's always handled over the phone, and the voices are usually different. They have no idea who I really am. And I always pay with cash."

"How often do you need these . . . adventures?"

"Once . . . sometimes twice a month," he said. "It's usually spur of the moment . . . when I need release from the stress of the job."

I wondered why he couldn't relax with a six-pack of Killian's Red or a jolt of Captain Morgan like the rest of us.

"What about the motel?" I asked.

"It's called the Wonderland. It's about forty miles from here . . . just off the thruway . . . the exit that has the big truck stop. They, uh . . . specialize in hourly rates."

My mind was racing with the conflicting emotions I felt. One part of me wanted to destroy him and maybe win Blair back after he was publicly burned at the stake. At the same time, I felt sorry for him. I reluctantly decided to give my better angels a chance.

"I'll start with the service," I said. "What did this girl call herself?"

"Why do you need to know that?"

"What am I supposed to do, Jordan, wave a magic wand?" I asked. "There is nothing else for me to go on. The only thing

I can think of to do is ask questions of everyone who might possibly be involved. Maybe if I ask enough questions, something will fall into place. I'll need the phone numbers of the call-girl service and the motel."

"Her name is Leila," he said, punching up the numbers on his phone. "And she isn't a call girl."

"Right. She's not a call girl. What room did you stay in this last time?" I asked.

"Room ten," he said, jotting the phone numbers down on a memo pad and handing them to me.

"You only have until tomorrow afternoon," he said as if I hadn't heard him the first time. "If you strike out, I'll submit my resignation and just pray the blackmailer doesn't go public."

"Yeah . . . keep praying. Am I working for you under the authority of the campus police department?" I asked.

He nodded.

"As quietly as possible."

"You'll need to clear my reinstatement with Morgo."

"Leave that to me," he said, picking up the phone. Flashing me one of the slow easy grins that had made so many women melt over the years, he added, "Thanks, Jake."

I was heading for the door when the sound of shouting erupted in the reception area outside his office. A moment later, the door burst open and a woman stormed into the room. I recognized her immediately, even without the straw hat. It was Evelyn Wheatley. Her eyes went straight to Jordan, who was still standing in front of Benjamin Franklin.

"Evelyn," he said as she advanced toward him. "I've left messages for you all morning. This is a terrible tragedy and . . ."

"You'd better do something right now," she demanded fiercely. "Dennis is dead, and no one here is doing a goddamn thing about it."

"We're doing everything we can," he said, reaching for her hand.

Ignoring it, she retorted, "I think there's some kind of cover-up going on."

Turning, she noticed me standing behind the open door. Her eyes widened as she pointed at me and said, "This officer suggested that Dennis might have been murdered. And when he raised that possibility to the moronic bitch who runs the campus police, she suspended him right in front of me. What's going on here?"

In response, Jordan looked over at me. Clearly what we had just discussed was off-limits.

"I'm not sure," I said finally. "But I don't believe he was on that bridge alone."

"Evelyn, I pledge to you that I will remain personally involved in this," Jordan said, guiding her over to the couch and sitting down beside her. "The investigation will be handled with every possible asset at our disposal, regardless of the cost."

As he tried to take her hand again, she batted his away.

"At least this officer has the intelligence to consider every possibility," she declared, pointing at me again. "Why isn't he in charge?"

"The college police have no official role in any criminal investigation," said Jordan, "but I will make sure he is assigned to the case as our liaison to the investigative team."

"I will not allow his death to be swept under the rug, no matter who might be embarrassed by the consequences," she said fiercely, getting up from the couch. "That woman even refused to allow me to see Dennis at the coroner's office. Please arrange for a car to take me there now."

"Of course," he said, quickly heading for his desk.

I hoped for Jordan's sake that the Groton Fire and Rescue Squad had been able to retrieve Wheatley's head. After he called the coroner and cleared her visit, Jordan's secretary escorted Evelyn Wheatley down to the parking lot.

"What a fucked-up mess," said Jordan when she was gone.

"Since Wheatley and his money seem to be the common denominator, I'm going to pursue both avenues and see where they lead. Aside from his wife, does Wheatley have any friends at the reunion that could have seen him in the final hours before the hanging?"

"I don't know. He was staying at his old fraternity house for homecoming weekend," said Jordan. "Some of his brothers from those days might have come back too."

"You should know there is a reporter tracking the story. Her name is Lauren Kenniston and she works for the *Groton Journal*. She was eavesdropping outside Morgo's office when I left to come over here."

"I've met her," said Jordan. "Grew up here, went to Princeton, and apparently had a promising career in fashion design in New York before tossing it in and moving back home."

"She left the bright city lights to come back here and cover Cub Scout blue and gold dinners?"

"I seem to recall some kind of family trouble."

"You need to call Captain Morgo," I said.

He picked up the telephone and dialed her extension.

"Janet," he began, "we have to rethink this Cantrell suspension."

I could hear her yelling through the line from across the room. They could have heard her in Buffalo.

6

I was walking out of the building when Jordan's green Volvo came swinging into the parking lot. Only one person could have been driving it. I found a vantage point to watch her from behind the colonnade that connected Jordan's building to the new performing arts center.

As Blair walked briskly toward the entrance, I felt the familiar electrical charge in my brain, all circuits flashing. In the years since we had been together, she had only grown more beautiful to me. Back then, her thick brown mane of hair had almost reached her waist. Now it was shoulder length, framing her face like a coronet as it swung back and forth in rhythm with her stride.

She was wearing a cream-colored dress with a cardigan sweater over it. I saw the familiar determined look on her face, the one that said I'm still going to change the world, as she disappeared into the building.

I was stunned at the raw impact she still had on me.

Since coming back to Groton, I had seen her only once, from a distance, but the feeling was exactly the same. I hadn't been prepared for it. Playing football, I had learned to brace myself when I saw a big linebacker coming at me. This was more like the times I was blindsided, taken out of a play from behind and rammed into the turf.

Walking over to the campus police building, I remembered the last time we were together, back when I thought we were going all the way. I had asked her to marry me again, but she repeated that it would be better to wait. I was on my five-day embarkation leave, and we were spending part of it at a small hotel in Saratoga Springs. We had just made love and were still lying together in the big four-poster bed.

I thought our lovemaking had a rightness about it, from the initial ferocity at the start of our relationship to the sensual growth that took place as we began to learn each other's mysteries, always wanting to give and receive pleasure until we were both fulfilled. Each completion would be followed by an interval of sweet, drowsy sleep until our sexual craving returned. I savored her body, and she proved beyond a doubt that she enjoyed mine.

On the last morning, we were having breakfast together after coming straight from bed.

"I love the feeling of power inside you, Jake, the physical hardness," she said at one point. "Your strength is . . . intoxicating. Yes . . . that would be the word for it."

I was about to thank her when she added, "But I can't believe that the man who made love to me the way you did last night could kill another human being."

"They murdered three thousand Americans, Blair," I said with honest conviction. "We are in a war over there. I've been trained to help fight it and to kill the enemy. They'll certainly be trying to kill me."

I had written my senior thesis on the just war theory and its advocacy by philosophers like Cicero and Thomas Aquinas, who personally found war morally abhorrent but understood it was sometimes necessary to wage it. I began trying to make the case that the war in Afghanistan met that test.

"What about the innocent people who get caught in the middle?" she asked.

"Innocent people always die in a war. It's an ugly business," I said.

"Then why do you have to do it?"

I didn't answer her. Looking back, I didn't have an answer. Blair let it drop.

Her first letters were filled with detailed and passionate observations of everything she was seeing and doing. She had started a new job with a nonprofit agency that worked with mentally challenged children, and she wrote eloquently of how one of the kids had worked against the odds to learn the alphabet.

Early on, there were also unabashed love letters, intimate and bawdy.

Other letters were filled with indignation. She wrote that apart from the military families bearing the burden of the war, there was no shared sacrifice, no sense that all Americans had a stake in it. I wrote back to her about the remarkable men I was serving with and how they were fighting for the right reasons.

I was still in Afghanistan when she wrote that she was taking another job. It was with a local community advocacy program that Jordan Langford had started in Detroit after he got back from the Peace Corps. She had heard about his work through one of our mutual friends and had written to him asking for a position. He told her to come on out.

Soon after that, her letters stopped coming.

A steady mass of St. Andrews alumni streamed past me as I arrived at the campus police building. The squad room was empty, as was the wire mesh holding pen. The lawyer in golf clothes had apparently sprung the two boys I had seen there earlier.

From my cubicle, I called Fred Beck, the local tow truck operator employed by the college to remove illegally parked cars. When he came on the line, I asked him to run my truck over to the Fall Creek Tavern. He was a regular there too.

"I knew that's what you would have wanted me to do, Jake," he said. "It's already in the Creeker parking lot."

When I got up to leave my cubicle, Captain Morgo was standing at the entrance.

"So you think you have an ace in the hole," she said, her voice husky. "Well that hole is disappearing fast, believe me."

"Why are you always so miserable?" I asked her.

"I despise you," she said. "I've tried to get rid of you from the day you first arrived."

"Why?"

"You already disgraced one uniform in Afghanistan, Cantrell. And then you thought you could just waltz back in here because you were a big football hero and a pal of the president."

"I guess you know everything about me."

"You were kicked out of the army. That tells it all. I can see the rot in your eyes."

There was no point in trying to give her my side of the story. She had already made up her mind. Like so many others.

"Yeah, that says it all."

"I've fought against the odds to earn every position I've had in law enforcement," she continued. "I've had to be tougher than a man in order to prove I could succeed in a man's profession. And now you have to poison my department."

I didn't bother to reply.

Resting one hand on the butt of her Glock 17, she said, "President Langford has asked that you be temporarily assigned as liaison to the sheriff's department while they continue to investigate the suicide of Dennis Wheatley. Sheriff Dickey has arranged to interview the friends and family of the deceased at the Tau Epsilon Rho fraternity at fourteen hundred this afternoon."

"I'll be there," I said.

"I don't give a shit what you do," said Captain Morgo. "As far as I'm concerned, you're still in a state of technical suspension.

Accordingly, you have no rights when it comes to preferred shift designations, and you do not have the privilege of wearing the uniform of this department. I do not expect to see you in this office, is that clear?"

I couldn't mask my smile.

"Go ahead and laugh," she said. "Your time is coming. Just this morning I received a complaint from a distinguished graduate of this college who claims you stole his camcorder and then physically threatened him. I urged him to press criminal charges against you."

When I didn't respond, she turned and marched back down the corridor, her heavy boots rapping like pistol shots on the polished floor. In the locker room, I changed into jeans, a blue work shirt, and a pair of old Rockports.

Leaving through the back door, I headed across campus. Like Mrs. Wheatley's dead husband, I now found myself at the end of a short rope. The only difference was that I still had my head.

At the moment, it wasn't cooperating with me. It wasn't even eleven o'clock, and I felt completely drained. I didn't know where to begin. The best idea I could come up with was to go back to bed and recharge my batteries, but I knew that wouldn't help the case. I decided to stimulate my muddled brain with black coffee.

I had passed the arts quad and was near the bridge when I suddenly felt like someone was following me. Call it an extra sense, but there was a time when I actually had one, and it was always triggered by the familiar prickling of the skin at the back of my neck. I stopped and turned around. No one was there. Another lost asset.

The bells on the library tower were chiming when I headed down the stone staircase that led to the footbridge. The yellow crime scene tape that had been strung across both ends had been removed, and nothing remained to suggest that something terrible had occurred there. So far, Jordan had been successful in keeping a lid on who had actually died. That would soon change when Lauren Kenniston filed her first story.

When I arrived at the Creeker, it was already packed with the Saturday morning crowd. A dozen customers had spilled out onto the side porch, drinking draft beer. Several of them waved a greeting as I went inside.

The tavern, a combination mountain lodge and old Adirondack boathouse, with rough-milled clapboard siding and big mullioned windows, had been there for more than a hundred years.

The main room had a high tin ceiling and a long oak-slab bar with traditional brass foot railings. Dusty hunting trophies adorned the walls, along with pictures of former St. Andrews sports heroes and long-dead customers. The owner rented out the upstairs rooms to students.

Since it was the closest watering hole to the campus, professors and students who needed a quick shot of confidence could get there between classes. At lunch it overflowed with blue-collar types—plumbers, electricians, and carpenters who worked on the campus construction projects and began their working days before sunrise.

I found an empty stool next to Ben Massengale. Even when the place was crowded, there was usually an empty stool alongside him. He rarely put in his upper bridge anymore and reeked from cigarettes and beer.

Looking at him as he tried to maintain his balance, it was hard to believe he was the same man I had met my first year at St. Andrews. Ben had commanded the ROTC battalion. Tall and rugged, he had won the Navy Cross at the Chosin Reservoir in Korea and was larger than life to those of us who went through the program. Now he lived off a small disability pension, and his shrunken cheeks were covered with several days' growth of gray beard. In spite of his age, his body retained a wiry toughness.

From the kitchen door, I could smell the aroma of French fries.

"Can I buy you a meal, Ben?" I asked.

He looked at me with moist eyes.

"Not hungry right now," he said as Kelly sailed into view behind the bar.

"You slay any dragons today?" she asked.

"I saw a couple," I said. "They weren't pretty."

"Sorry," she said. "What are you having?"

In her forties, she still maintained the figure that had once graced *Playboy* in one of the college spreads featuring bare-assed girls from the different football conferences. Kelly was wearing a short-sleeved crimson shirt over skin-tight red bullfighter pants.

She was a sun worshipper and her skin was a rich golden brown, which dramatically set off her naturally blonde hair.

"Black coffee," I said.

She glanced at me in surprise.

"I'm working."

"Coffee it is," she said, moving off.

I saw someone trying to open one of the back windows in the bar that hung over the edge of the gorge. The window had been nailed shut after a drunk had fallen through it to his death. The recollection brought my mind back to why Dennis Wheatley would have been on the footbridge if he was afraid of heights. No answer came to me.

I was finishing my second cup of coffee when I heard nervous giggling behind me and turned to see four slumming angels in the space behind us. That's what Kelly called them, St. Andrews coeds who thought it was cool to occasionally drink with the peasants before heading back to their dorm or sorority house. They were standing together in an awkward circle, sipping long-neck bottles of Labatt Blue and gazing around the bar as if we were zoo animals.

"So what do you do?" one of them asked me.

"I just escaped from Auburn State Prison," I said.

One of the girls giggled again. Sipping his shot of rye, Ben managed to swing around on his stool without falling off and said, "Honey, I'm ninety-four fucking years old."

"You don't look a day over three hundred," said the girl, grinning back at her friends.

"On this day in 1943, I was on the canal," he came back at her.

"What canal?" asked the coed as Kelly set another mug of coffee in front of me.

"The canal . . . Second Marine Raiders. We knocked their Jap asses back at the Tenaru River . . . to Red Mike Edson," he said, raising his empty glass in salute.

"You fought what today?" she asked.

"The goddamn Japs," said Ben.

One of the girls visibly recoiled. She looked Japanese.

"You should be ashamed of yourself. That's a racial slur," declared one of her friends.

"What canal is he talking about?" repeated the first girl.

"Guadalcanal," said a gray-haired man sitting on the other side of Ben. "Colonel Mike Edson commanded the Marine Raiders at Bloody Ridge."

"That's right," agreed Ben, nodding. "Best goddamn marine I ever served under."

The gray-haired man was wearing an old army field jacket. Unlike the ones kids buy at the army surplus outlets, this one still had patches on it, including the Vietnam combat badge. The Creeker drew a lot of retired military men.

"Where is Guadalcanal?" asked the girl.

"A different universe," said the Vietnam veteran.

The slumming angels briefly huddled together before moving out in tight formation through the exit door to the side porch.

"Goddamn . . . I still like the young ones," said Ben glumly as he watched them go.

I turned back to Kelly, who had just poured a couple of fingers of something into a small tumbler. She set it in front of me and said, "I think you might need this."

I looked down into the dark-amber fluid. I knew exactly what it was. I could see the Smoky Mountains of Tennessee in one of the little bubbles that frothed near the top of the glass. The home place of Sergeant Alvin York. Generations of mountain men had labored very hard to bring this elixir to me. I thought about everything I was supposed to be doing and knew it was a mistake to take the first sip.

I held the glass up to my nose. The fragrance rose toward the back of my sinus passages and met my brain. I downed the two fingers of George Dickel sour mash in one long swallow. A moment later, I felt its warmth heading south with a kick to my heart and then down to my stomach. I carefully placed the tumbler back on the bar and looked up at Kelly's big brown eyes.

"How was that?" she asked.

"Christmas morning," I said.

My mind was suddenly focusing better. There was a distinct clarity to all the sounds and smells that hadn't been there before. I knew that another one would probably clear my mind even further and nodded at Kelly to pour it.

I took my time with the second. Two swallows. When I had finished it, my mind was like a steel trap, and my energy level was growing by the minute. It occurred to me that I should phone the call-girl service and try to arrange a meeting with the one Jordan knew as Leila.

I pulled out my cell phone and walked outside to find a quiet place to make the call. While I was keying in the number, it struck me that if the blackmailer was part of the call-girl operation, he would know that Jordan had received the video recording in the mail and would never set up another date. There was a danger that I would blow the thing sky high. At the same time, I didn't have any other options.

The number rang three times.

"Friends with All the Benefits," said a sultry female voice. She was probably seventy years old and weighed four hundred pounds.

"This is Alicia Verlaine," I said.

There was a pause, and I could hear keys clicking on a word processor or laptop.

"Welcome back, dear," she said without a trace of surprise. "Can I arrange an appointment for you?"

Thanks to the sour mash, I remembered that the sheriff had scheduled interviews with Dennis Wheatley's friends and fraternity brothers for two o'clock at Tau Epsilon Rho.

"Seven o'clock this evening," I said. "Same place as always."

"Certainly," replied the woman. "Any special requests?"

"I was hoping to meet Leila again."

"May I put you on hold, dear?"

"Sure."

Two minutes passed before she was back again.

"Leila is not available this evening," she informed me, "but I notice in our file that you have enjoyed two appointments with Jana. She's on call this evening."

"I'd prefer to see Leila again," I said, adding a distinct whine to my voice. "Would she be available at double the regular friendly gift?"

"Please hold on again," said the sultry voice with a low chuckle.

Leila must have been connected to a pager or a cell phone. I wondered what she did when she wasn't having orgasms at the end of a vibrator. This time the voice was back in thirty seconds.

"Yes, Leila could rearrange her schedule for you."

Good old capitalism at its best.

"Great," I said. "I'll see her there, and thanks."

After I hung up with the call-girl service, I entered the number for the motel. "Wonderland," said a male voice. "Buntid speaking."

"I need a room for tonight. Around six thirty."

"For how long?" he asked.

"About two hours," I replied, figuring that would give me plenty of time to check out how the video recording had been done and to have a productive chat with Leila.

"We rent by the hour. An hour's fifty bucks," he said.

"An hour then," I said, not having a hundred bucks. I wanted at least twenty minutes to look over the room before she got there. Assuming she was on time, I would have only thirty minutes to talk with her in the room. I could always finish the conversation in my truck. It occurred to me that I had no money to pay her either.

"Is room ten available?"

"Yeah . . . in about twenty minutes," he said.

"At six thirty."

"Don't worry . . . we got plenty of rooms."

"I wanted that one," I pressed. "I like the view."

"The view?" he growled. "Ten looks over the diesel pumps."

"It reminds me of home," I growled back at him.

There was silence for five seconds. Apparently, I had touched his heart.

"All right . . . I'll make a note," he said as if he were saving me the Warren Buffett suite at the Waldorf Astoria. I was glad he didn't ask for a credit card number to secure it. I didn't have one anymore.

My third call was to Jordan. The first thing he asked me was whether I had any leads. That's what desperation does to otherwise intelligent people. I told him I needed two hundred bucks in cash for working capital, and he said he would have someone bring it right over.

When I got back to the bar, Ben Massengale was gone and the prefootball game crowd was thinning out. The Vietnam veteran had left too. His stool had been taken by Johnny Joe Splendorio, another regular.

"How they hangin', Jake?" he asked as I sat.

"Fine," I said, looking down the bar for Kelly.

She was already on her way back with two more fingers of sour mash. A Clara Barton for the ages was Kelly. Johnny Joe peered at me through gimlet eyes as I knocked it down.

About fifty, he carefully patted the dozen strands of hair that were lacquered across his scalp and said, "I've written a new song, Jake . . . another hit . . . I mean this one is guaranteed."

Johnny Joe claimed to have written several country-western songs that had made the charts. No one had ever heard of any of them. He was always looking for someone to back him in another try for Nashville greatness.

"Congratulations," I said.

"You got friends, Jake. I mean you know people."

I knew better than to say anything. It would only encourage him.

"This one is really good," he added with the familiar grinding sound.

Johnny Joe had a serious chin tick that moved his teeth dramatically to the left as he ground his jaw together. It wasn't pleasant to look at. My eyes happened to catch the photograph of me over the bar. It was shoe-horned between several others. We had been playing Tulane for the national championship, and I had just broken through the line with thirty seconds left in the game. The kid in the picture was a stranger to me.

"It's called 'Jesus, My Semi, and Me.'"

I happened to be looking down at the floor as a construction worker on the next stool removed his steel-toed boot from the brass foot railing, leaving the crusty outline of a muddy boot print.

"See, this ol' trucker fella is hauling a load of frozen hog bellies in the middle of the night from Muncie, Indiana," went on Johnny Joe, his face alive with excitement. "He goes through this dense fog, see . . . and when he comes out the other side, his eighteen-wheeler is comin' up Calvary Hill, and the Romans are about to nail Jesus up on the cross. Can you see it?"

In my mind's eye, I could see Dennis Wheatley walking on the edge of the bridge railing. Based on the patterns of the dirt marks I had seen, he had probably made it ten feet before falling to his death.

"The truck driver's got an M-4 on his gun rack, see?" said Johnny Joe. "He comes down out of the cab with it and just cuts loose. The chorus goes like this: *I killed me some Romans and I killed me some Jews. Now me and Jesus are spreading the news.*"

If Wheatley's wife was telling the truth about his being afraid of heights, it must have been pure torture for him. Why would a man dying of pancreatic cancer who didn't drink and was acrophobic be walking on the edge of that railing while drunk?

"He saves Jesus, see?" said Johnny Joe, showing a hint of frustration.

"Yeah, I see," I said, losing my train of thought.

"I know it needs work," he went on, "but the important stuff is all there."

Kelly appeared again in front of me as Johnny Joe spotted Pete Sarkus coming in the door and moved off to put the bite on him. I decided to have a last hit of George Dickel to help me unravel the mystery a bit further. The tumbler was almost half full when she set it down on the bar.

I closed my eyes and tried to focus on the questions I needed to ask Dennis Wheatley's friends at two o'clock. Like where they had been all night. Unfortunately, the mind-boggling image of Jordan in his red lace lingerie kept ruining my concentration. When I reached down for the glass again, it was empty.

"You want to join me on my shift break?" Kelly asked on her next pass.

"Can't," I said, my brain turning to suet. "Have a lot to do today."

She glared up at me as she cleared the bottles and glasses that littered the bar like spent ammunition.

"I'm going on break," she repeated. "This is your last chance."

I probably should have felt guilty for getting drunk instead of helping out my friend. As they say, bad habits die hard. We were heading out the door when the student intern with the purple streak down the middle of her scalp arrived from Jordan's office. She handed me a sealed envelope. I put it in my hip pocket and thanked her for bringing it over.

7

You stupid asshole, I thought to myself. I was reasonably sober again, and we were lying naked together in Kelly's queen-sized bed along with her menagerie of stuffed animals.

"All I want is for life to be like *Pretty Woman*," said Kelly, leaning over to nuzzle my throat.

It was a movie she watched at least once a month, crying at the sappiest moments as if they were cherished friends she hadn't seen for years.

"I have to go," I said.

We had started sleeping together in the summer. Her car salesman husband had decided she was aging too fast and was in the process of trading her in for a younger model. But the imperfections that bothered him only made her seem more attractive to me. The creases around her eyes, the wrinkles, the slightly sagging skin along her jawline all made her seem more vulnerable and real.

It had seemed fine at the beginning. She was personally very tidy. Her house was immaculate. She didn't smoke or chew tobacco. She had a good sense of humor and a good laugh. She took good care of her cat. Her house plants were healthy. She was honest. She worked out all the time. She was a good lover.

I silently added up all the things I had learned since. Even though she had a good sense of humor, she could never laugh at herself. She had a "thing" about black people. She hadn't read a book since high school. I wasn't sure if she had ever read one. Up to the moment she fell asleep, she never stopped talking. It was as if any elapsed quiet time between us aside from sex might cause the end of the world. Her favorite subjects were soap operas and bodily functions. She hated jazz and classical music. Her television set was always on, even if she wasn't home. The only thing she knew how to cook was chili.

"My lawsuit is going forward," she said.

"That's great," I said.

"The Razzano brothers have agreed to represent me," she went on. Rolling on top of me, she straddled my hips and added, "I'm going to sue the hell out of them, Jake."

Kelly had interviewed a few months earlier for a hostess position at a Hustler's restaurant near Binghamton. Like Hooters, it specialized in amply endowed waitresses. After being turned down, she became convinced that it was a case of age discrimination.

"Are these anything to be ashamed of?" she demanded, fondling her breasts as if they were Fabergé eggs.

"No," I agreed.

When it came to breasts, Kelly's were spectacular. Even in her forties, they rose heavenward like twin sidewinder missiles.

"Hustlers only hire children with big tits," she said angrily, "and that's wrong."

She lowered herself toward me and nestled into my arms. As her erect nipples grazed my chest, she slid me inside her again. Her hair covered my eyes, blotting out the sunlight from the window.

She began to ride me with a leisurely, measured rhythm. By the time we reached climax, the two of us were thrashing around the bed like rabbits in a snare, her lips locked onto mine and her tongue at the back of my throat. After my heart stopped pounding, I tumbled back into a black hole.

I was awakened by the sound of garbage cans being over-turned in the alley behind her apartment. When I opened my eyes, Kelly's face was a few inches from mine. Droplets of sweat dotted her forehead. She used her fingertips to sweep away the tendrils of blonde hair that covered her eyes. Her hot moist skin was still adhered to mine.

"I love you, Jake," she whispered. "If you marry me, I'll fuck you like this every day and night."

I glanced at my watch. It was two fifteen.

"Shit," I said, sitting up.

Her eyes filled with tears. It was pointless to explain that I was already late for the sheriff's interviews. She had heard too many different excuses in recent months to believe me anymore.

"You're already married," I said, putting on my socks.

"I meant after," she said earnestly. "You deserve to be happy, Jake. You were so depressed when I met you. I could make you happy. I know it. I so love you, baby."

She was waiting for me to repeat the love word back to her. That word so often used to rationalize basic sexual needs, the poetic justification for millions of desperate couplings every minute all over the world. I had given love once, and Blair had thrown it away.

At the same time, I despised myself for what I had become. I knew I had given Kelly pleasure, just as she had me. We shared the same desperate hunger. But for my part, it was no more than the need for intimacy, the temporary pushing back against the loneliness of the spirit, cornering it for a time in a dark place while we were joined together. When it was over, Kelly and I were lonely strangers lying in the same perfumed bed surrounded by her stuffed animals.

"I've got to go," I said.

As soon as I stood up, my headache kicked in again with a vengeance. Glancing momentarily into the gilt mirror as I went past, I thought that I could actually see my head throbbing. Usually, my headaches built like a slowly developing storm front. This one was coming on fast. I could feel it gathering strength in my sinus cavities and behind both eyes.

Kelly kept a full supply of headache, back ache, and female remedies in her medicine chest. I swallowed four extrastrength Tylenol tablets with a glass of Alka-Seltzer and stepped into the shower. I kept it at the hottest setting for as long as I could and then adjusted the faucet to full cold.

Ten minutes later, I was out the front door and headed on foot for Tau Epsilon Rho.

8

Dennis Wheatley's fraternity house was a throwback to the grandiose times in the 1920s, when major movie production companies were based in Groton before Hollywood took hold of the industry.

Early film producers had been drawn by the dramatic backdrop of waterfalls and deep gorges. Derring-do serials like *The Perils of Pauline*, the kind of stuff where the damsel is tied to the railroad tracks by the villain and saved by the hero, had been shot here.

A couple of the early movie moguls had foolishly decided to build lavish homes in town, and after the movie business died, one of them had eventually become the Tau Epsilon Rho fraternity. It was a four-story pile of stone with leaded casement windows, *Wuthering Heights* chimneys, and a dramatic view of Groton Lake.

As I was walking across the far end of the campus, I heard a howling roar from the football stadium and realized the homecoming game was in progress. I thought back to the years when

Jordan and I were the tandem backs on two undefeated teams and had both been showered with fleeting glory. It had all been so trivial.

When I arrived at the frat house, a touch football game was taking place on the expansive lawn. The players had gone to the trouble of marking off the sidelines with orange construction cones.

"You only tagged me with one hand," screamed the player holding the football after an apparent touchdown run.

"I got you with both," shouted another player.

They were all trying to prove they hadn't lost a step since college. A cafeteria table covered with a white tablecloth stood at the fifty yard line. Behind it, two winsome young women were filling green plastic reunion cups with draft beer from a metal keg. Several dozen spectators were doing their best to keep the cups empty.

The side parking lot of the fraternity house had several million dollars' worth of cars in it. A lone Ford pickup was parked behind the dumpster near the back entrance to the kitchen. It was probably the cook's.

Checking my watch as I went through the ornamental iron gates flanking the entrance, I saw that I was only thirty minutes late. A deputy sheriff was standing in the front foyer talking into a handheld radio.

"What's the score?" he asked whoever was on the other end. When he punched the device to receive, I could hear the bellowing of the football crowd over at the crescent.

"We're down two points with ten minutes to go in the quarter," said a voice over the clamoring noise. "Durbin just got intercepted again."

The deputy waved me down the carved mahogany staircase that led to the fraternity's chapter room. There, a group of older alumni stood solemnly in the corridor just outside the closed entrance doors. Waiting in a ragged line, they ranged in age from forty to senility. Two of the women were dabbing at tears with handkerchiefs.

Another uniformed deputy was standing guard at the doors. As I came up, he motioned for the man at the head of the line to go inside. I showed him my campus security badge and he let me through.

The chapter room was about fifty feet square with hand-hewn beams on the ceilings and a fireplace large enough to hold an Abrams tank. I assumed it was used for special occasions like donkey basketball games and torturing new pledges. Hiking across the parquet tiles, I imagined decades of pledges, stripped naked and scrubbing the floor with toothbrushes in order to earn the privilege of becoming a member.

At the far end of the room, a cluster of people stood near leather armchairs that faced a picture window overlooking the lake. Three plainclothes investigators from the sheriff's department were conducting interviews with individual alumni at the mahogany library tables.

I saw Evelyn Wheatley in the group near the window. Standing next to her was a tall, distinguished-looking man wearing a gray suit with a white shirt and black clerical collar. Nearby, Sheriff Jim Dickey was talking to a florid woman in a pink sun suit. Seeing me coming, he excused himself from the woman and came strutting toward me.

"Glad you could spare the time to make it on over here, Soldier," he said. "Sorry we couldn't wait on you."

American flag patches were sewed onto both arms of his khaki uniform blouse, and another was emblazoned on the crown of the Smokey the Bear hat he held in his hand.

"I'm also working on another case," I said.

"It got big tits?" Dickey came back with a toothy grin.

He was still sheriff because the rednecks in the rural parts of the county kept voting to reelect him by overwhelming margins. According to Jordan Langford, his slogan in the last campaign pointed out that "Groton is two square miles surrounded by reality." He would have been popular in any rural county of Mississippi back in the 1950s.

"You goin' ta seed, Soldier," said Big Jim. "You be sproutin' gin blossoms pretty soon. But don't worry. We got everything under control here. My people have already interviewed everyone who was stayin' in the alumni wing last night. Most of 'em was snug in their beds when the fella decided to end it all."

"Someone was out there on that bridge to help him," I said.

He shook his head with a condescending smile.

Dickey's standard approach for intimidating people was to get right in their face, just as he was doing now. His breath reeked from whatever he had eaten at lunch. Maybe he thought it was going to make me faint.

"My people still say suicide," he said. "The word on Wall Street is that Wheatley's company was in trouble."

"You have friends on Wall Street?"

"I could grow to really dislike you, son. Good thing you're on your way out over there and I don't have to waste my time. Ol' Morgo told me you're about two inches from sucking eggs."

"From what my people tell me, two inches is all you've got, Jim."

"I have a feeling you'll be paying us a visit out at my jail one of these days," he said menacingly. "Just keep on giving me shit . . . I'll make you feel right at home when you get there."

"You'll take my shit as long as the widow decides to keep me involved in the investigation," I shot back. "A billion dollars brings a lot of spank, doesn't it, Sheriff?"

"He was just another jumper as far as I'm concerned," he said, poking me hard in the chest. "Probably had faggot problems like the last one."

When he lowered his meaty shoulder, I saw Evelyn Wheatley approaching us.

"Thank you for coming, Officer Cantrell," she said with a bright artificial smile.

In Afghanistan, I had witnessed a similar reaction from a tribal chieftain after his youngest son had been murdered in an ancient border dispute. Until he had exacted his revenge on the neighboring clan leader, he acted as if the world were his oyster and the loss of his son no more consequential than the death of a piece of favored livestock.

She had changed into a tailored beige pantsuit, and her black hair was woven into a French braid. She looked like exactly who she was, the determined wife of a billionaire who could steam-roll anyone who stood in her path. At the moment, she was all take-charge. The grieving would come later.

"I already informed Sheriff Dickey that I have retained the AuCoin Investigative Agency in New York City to represent my interests in this matter. Les AuCoin is sending a team of his best investigators up here to assist you. I hope that you will give them your full cooperation."

"Anything I can do to help, ma'am," said Big Jim, pivoting to stand over her.

"Thank you, Sheriff," she said, dismissing him with a low-voltage smile, "but I was talking to Officer Cantrell."

Taking my hand, she led me toward the gray-suited man in the clerical collar standing in front of the picture window.

"What is your first name?" she asked me.

"Jake."

"Jake Cantrell, this is my friend Robin Massey. Robin . . . this is the officer I spoke to you about. He believes Dennis might have been murdered."

He looked me directly in the eyes. His handshake was firm and dry.

"I'm very sorry that we have to meet under these circum-stances," he said in a honey-rich baritone.

"Robin was my husband's closest friend and roommate when they were students here at St. Andrews. He remains Dennis's closest friend to this day," said Evelyn Wheatley, ignoring the inaccurate tense.

At one time, the Reverend Massey had probably enjoyed a full head of red hair. It was now reddish-gray and combed straight back from the crown of his distinguished forehead.

"I will miss him more than I can say, Evelyn," he said.

There was nothing remotely evangelical about him. I had met plenty of five-star evangelists at Benning and other places I had served. He wasn't like them. There was an almost serene grace in his manner.

"Robin runs a halfway house for alcoholics and drug addicts in St. Louis," added Mrs. Wheatley. "He has devoted most of his adult life to this cause. Dennis was one of his biggest supporters. He will tell you that Dennis would never take his own life."

Reverend Massey nodded in agreement.

"Sheriff Dickey and that Captain Morgo refuse to accept anything we've told them," she said. "That's why I've retained the AuCoin agency."

"They don't want it to be murder," I said. "I'm sure you can understand why."

She nodded almost violently and said, "I don't care who gets hurt. I want to know the truth."

"I'll share everything I've learned with them as soon as they arrive," I said.

"Thank you," she replied as a woman came up behind her and began sobbing. Evelyn Wheatley turned to greet her with a warm hug and a smile.

Looking back at Reverend Massey, I remembered Lieutenant Ritterspaugh talking earlier that morning about my aura. This guy definitely had one. His brown eyes seemed to radiate goodness, and there was no affectation in them.

"When did you arrive back in Groton?" I asked him.

"Yesterday afternoon. I flew into LaGuardia from St. Louis on Thursday evening. Dennis and Evelyn picked me up at the airport, and I spent the night at their home in Mamaroneck. We drove up here together yesterday."

"You roomed together with him at St. Andrews?"

"For the last three years we were here."

"Just the two of you?"

"Our senior year, Hoyt Palmer lived with us in the big suite on the top floor."

"Did he come back here for homecoming weekend too?"

"He did," said Robin Massey, "all the way from Helsinki, Finland. The three of us started planning this visit last year."

"Is he here now?" I asked, glancing around.

"Hoyt isn't feeling well. His wife said he was vomiting most of the night and is very dehydrated. Possibly something he ate on the plane."

"When was the last time you saw Mr. Wheatley alive?" I asked.

"About midnight . . . shortly before I went to bed."

"Did he say if he was planning to go out?"

"No, he didn't."

"What was his mood at that time?"

"He was fine—relaxed and glad to be back here with us for the reunion."

"To your knowledge, did he have any enemies here in Groton?"

He paused again and stared out the window at the lake. He was the kind of man who thought through an important question before answering.

"None that I know of," he said firmly. "Here or anywhere else. On top of everything else in his life, Dennis was the chairman of the St. Andrews Board of Trustees. One of his passions was planning projects to help the college as well as several local organizations in the memory of distinguished alumni from the college's past."

Massey's eyes suddenly went south for a moment before they came back to meet mine.

"What are you thinking?" I asked him.

"Nothing, really," he said. "Old memories."

"To your knowledge, was he unhappy about anything?"

He shook his head and said, "Dennis was very high on life . . . about the things he could accomplish with the great fortune he had been blessed to achieve."

Obviously, Massey didn't know about Wheatley's cancer either.

"That's another thing . . . his entire fortune was earned through an idea he had conceived to help our society . . . to help people eat healthier and enjoy a better quality of life. His whole life since college has been focused on helping others."

"That's just what Mrs. Wheatley said about yours."

"In much smaller ways," he said. "Infinitely smaller."

"Have you ever had military training?" I asked.

"No. Why do you ask?"

"Just curious."

"After graduation, I served in the Peace Corps in India and then worked at a street clinic in Calcutta for eleven years before coming home," he said. "Sometimes Calcutta felt like a combat zone," he added with a wry smile.

"I understand," I said, and I did, having once hidden out in the untouchables' quarter of Kabul for a week. "What about Mr. Palmer?"

"Hoyt never joined the military either," said Robin Massey. "Like me, he had the wanderlust. For him it was Europe. He's lived in Helsinki for the last twenty years."

"What does he do?"

"Hoyt Palmer is representative of an expression they use over there," said Massey. "He's as talkative as a Finn . . . which of course means just the opposite. For the last ten years, he has run a nonprofit environmental organization dedicated to protecting the wildlands in the north."

"Another do-gooder," I said, smiling.

"We've all tried," he said as Sheriff Dickey came up to us. He bulled in close enough to crowd us both back a step.

"When do I get to talk to this other roommate?" he asked Massey, glancing down at his watch.

"His wife, Inge, told me an hour ago that he might have to go to the hospital," said the minister. "Apparently he is quite ill."

"From what she said, sounds like it might be food poisoning," offered the sheriff. "Anyone else in your group gotten sick?"

"Not that I'm aware of."

"I meant to ask you something," said the sheriff to Robin Massey. "You married?"

"No," said Massey, grinning. "I guess I never found a woman who would put up with me."

The attempt at humor was lost on Dickey. He leaned in closer and said, "No offense intended here, Padre, but as far as you know, are there any homo connections to this thing?"

"I'm not a homosexual if that's what you mean," said Massey, color rising in his cheeks. "And neither was Dennis."

"Don't get me wrong," said Big Jim. "I've got nothing against them, but we had a suicide at that same bridge last year that turned out to be queer."

"Don't misjudge my faith for weakness," declared Massey. "If you continue to harass Evelyn or me with these innuendoes, I'll come back here for your next reelection campaign and use all the Wheatley family resources to organize an effort to defeat you. Is that clear enough?"

Dickey's chin began bobbing up and down like a mario-
nette as Massey stalked off to rejoin Evelyn Wheatley in front of
the picture window. When they both turned to glare at him, he
flashed them a grisly smile.

The plainclothes deputies who had interviewed Wheatley's
fellow alumni in the fraternity had just finished their work, and
I went over to talk to them. No one had seen Wheatley leave the
fraternity house the previous night. Mrs. Wheatley had stated
she'd gone to bed around ten. The last person who reported seeing Wheatley was an octogenarian alumnus who happened to
be reading in the library at around midnight. According to him,
Wheatley had been his usual enthusiastic self, stopping to ask
if the old man was enjoying his time back at St. Andrews. They
chatted for several minutes before he left the library.

I decided to wait to see whether Hoyt Palmer would feel well
enough to talk to us. In the meantime, a preliminary report
arrived from the county coroner. The fire and rescue team had
found Dennis Wheatley's head wedged between two boulders in
the gorge. Until an autopsy took place, it would be impossible
for him to closely estimate the time of death. His best guess was
that Wheatley had died somewhere between two and five in the
morning. At the time of death, his blood-alcohol level was .31,
more than three times the legal limit.

Once they got into the autopsy, they would also find the
cancer.

None of it appeared to fit. According to his wife, he didn't
drink alcohol and had never done so during their twenty-year

marriage. The man was acrophobic, and yet he had climbed onto the railing of the bridge with a concertina snare around his neck and managed to keep his balance for almost ten feet before he fell. Someone had cut the telephone line at the blue emergency box. It obviously wasn't Dennis Wheatley.

Something about the intricately braided rope was familiar to me, but I couldn't remember where I might have seen it before. The use of concertina wire suggested a military connection, but a lot of other people had access to that stuff these days. I had seen it at a local construction site.

I doubted whether Robin Massey had anything to do with Wheatley's death, but that didn't mean he wasn't in possession of information that might help solve the mystery. Possibly he didn't realize the importance of what he knew. I rarely recognized the importance of what I knew anymore. What I really needed was another hit of George Dickel sour mash.

The late October sun was slanting harshly through the windows, bringing with it an unnatural humidity that foretold the approach of Hurricane Ilse. I went out to the front lawn to get some fresh air.

The touch football game had ended. No one had bothered to pick up the construction cones on the lawn. The metal keg of beer was still sitting on the cafeteria table along the sideline. The ground was littered with empty cups. I picked one up and filled it from the tap. The beer was still cold.

I looked at my watch. It was almost four o'clock, and I needed to leave for the Wonderland Motel by six if I was going to have enough time to search the room before Leila arrived. As I placed the still-full cup back on the table, I heard the wail of an emergency siren coming toward the house.

An ambulance pulled up at the front entrance. When I got there, two emergency medical technicians were rolling a gurney out the front door. A man was lying on it, his chest and legs strapped tight to the frame. His eyes were closed, his face pallid and slack-jawed. That was all I saw before they lifted him into the back. Robin Massey was standing under the front portico as the ambulance headed off with its siren blaring. I walked over to him.

"Hoyt Palmer?" I asked.

"Yes. Apparently his blood pressure was dangerously low."

One of the sheriff's squad cars was still parked in the turnaround. The front passenger door was open, and a deputy was sitting in the front seat listening to the football game on the radio. A tremendous roar went up from the stadium that we could hear all the way across the campus, and the deputy started pounding the dashboard.

"He's in . . . he's in!" shouted the announcer over the crowd.

As I turned to walk back to my truck, I heard another voice behind me.

"You're not in uniform, Officer Cantrell."

It was the reporter, Lauren Kenniston. She was wearing a rain jacket over tightly fitted corduroys, boots, and a red flannel shirt. Her auburn hair was hidden under a New York Mets cap.

"This is a new design we're testing out," I said. "Makes it easier to blend in with the criminal element."

"We should compare notes on the Wheatley killing. Looks like it's going to be quite a story."

I decided she didn't have anything I didn't have. At least not yet.

"I don't have any notes," I said.

"I gather you have balls," she said.

I was in enough trouble and didn't respond.

She pulled a card out of her jacket and handed it to me.

"Text me if you need anything," she said with a grin.

I took it and headed over to my truck.

9

Bug was waiting for me when I opened the cabin door. When our eyes met, she heaved a long martyred sigh, as if my leaving her behind each day would eventually weigh on my conscience for eternity.

I headed into the kitchen. Opening the refrigerator door, I stuck my head inside the freezer compartment and relaxed for a moment as the cold air cooled my face. At the back of the freezer, I noticed the braised sirloin tips in wine sauce that I had made for Bug earlier in the week and frozen in individual plastic containers.

Removing two containers, I pulled off the tops and put them into the microwave for four minutes. Opening the large container of garlic-flavored brown rice I made for her each week and kept in the vegetable drawer, I dumped three handfuls into the top of a double-boiler saucepan. After running tap water into the base pan, I set it at low heat on the gas stove.

Bug began to bark at the front door. Opening it, I saw the mailman driving away in his little carrier van. I brought the mail back inside and quickly sorted it on the kitchen counter. A utility bill, a monthly bank statement confirming my checking account balance of 243 dollars, and a couple of catalogues.

Stripping off my clothes, I took a quick shower under the lukewarm flow from the cold faucet. By the time I had dried myself, the food was ready. I served Bug's dinner in her two favorite bowls, the first holding the braised beef tips and the second the steamed brown rice. She never liked the meal mixed together. I waited for her to take the first exploratory nibble before heading into my bedroom to get dressed.

There was a clean pair of jeans in the bureau, and I put them on along with a white polo shirt and my old desert boots. Having no idea what might be waiting for me at the Wonderland Motel, I removed the army-issue Colt .45 from its hiding place in the crawl space next to the chimney and checked the magazine. It was full.

I decided to use a shoulder harness under my blazer, but when I finished dressing, it didn't feel right. For one thing, I had lost a lot of weight since leaving the army, and my chest disappeared under the loose-fitting folds of the jacket. Recalling the slight Eurasian-looking girl I had seen in Jordan's video recording, I decided she didn't warrant a .45 and put the pistol back in its hiding place.

Walking through the kitchen, I glanced down at Bug's food bowls and noticed that the one holding the sirloin tips had been licked clean. More than half the brown rice in the other bowl was gone too. She was lying on her Indian throw rug in the living room, licking her front paws.

"I suppose some alien abducted your dinner, huh?" I said with a superior grin.

She gave me a baleful stare before continuing to clean her muzzle with the back of her front paw. Making sure that the screen door to the porch was still propped open, I went out to the truck. A light breeze was pushing heavy air off the lake.

As I reached the pickup, I heard movement behind me, and Bug appeared at my side. Her bushy white tail was wagging with excitement as she waited for me to open the door to the cab. *What the hell*, I thought, and decided to take her with me.

Until about a year ago, I would just open the door and she would soar up five feet into the cab and land on her cushion with room to spare. Since then, she had lost all the spring in her hind legs. In my mind's eye, I remembered the time near Kandahar when she leaped from a running position over a six-foot-high stone stockade wall. I was right behind her and had to use both hands to vault over it. We had both lost a few steps since.

When I opened the driver's-side door, she took off feebly from the ground. I immediately placed my hands under her chest and belly and propelled her up and onto the passenger seat. Humiliated, she turned to glare at me before shaking her hips and settling on her cushion.

Starting the truck, I headed out to the lake road and stopped. There were two routes I could take up to the motel. The first led through town past the campus and followed a state highway most of the way. The other route ran north along the lake. It was a bit longer, but there was always less traffic, and the view was spectacular.

As I drove north, the autumn colors blazed before me in a pageant of red, orange, and gold. They were no more vivid than the mental image of Jordan in his lingerie and the memory of Dennis Wheatley's head disappearing over the falls. I wondered again if the two events could somehow be connected. Wheatley's money.

Realizing I hadn't eaten all day, I stopped at a Quik Mart near the turnoff to Romulus and bought myself a roast beef hero and twenty ounces of coffee. Spreading the butcher paper on my lap, I slowly ate the sandwich as the country road veered left away from the lake and cut northwest through old-growth forest toward Rochester.

Maybe ten minutes later, I realized that the sky had gotten progressively darker. I craned my head out the window for a moment. To the south, massive thunderheads had turned the sky leaden gray. They seemed to be hovering right over the treetops.

As I came out of the forest into an open stretch of country road, a brutal gust of wind shook the cab of the truck and pushed me toward the gravel apron. I had been through several hurricanes during the years I was stationed at Fort Benning, and they were always preceded by the same heavy air, the same teasing gusts of harsh wind. It remained to be seen whether this was going to be a bad one after it had traveled all the way up the Alleghenies.

A spatter of rain hit the windshield and stopped as quickly as it came. I turned on the radio to find out if there was a new forecast, but it gave out only a burst of static.

Twenty miles farther up the road, I began to see the signs for the New York State Thruway. The darkening sky began spitting rain again as I arrived at a neon light stanchion that rose thirty feet up in the air. Glowing red letters spelled out the word "Wonderland."

I recalled reading in an old state police report that the Wonderland had been built by one of the New York organized crime families back in the 1970s when they thought they had bought off enough state politicians to bring legalized casino gambling up here. The hoods turned out to be right, although their timing was off by forty years, and they didn't anticipate that the casinos would be owned by much older families like the Mohawks and the Iroquois.

The three-story motel complex looked as if it had been designed by the same people who built the early casinos in Vegas. The front portico of the central building was adorned with gigantic fluted columns, each one painted to look like a peppermint stick.

A circular concrete fountain in the shape of a Roman bath stood forlornly in the middle of the cracked, tar-surfaced turnaround, its modern nymphs ready to spew water into the surrounding grotto if someone turned on the water again. The empty grotto was littered with beer cans and old racing forms from Vernon Downs.

There was also a big truck stop next to the motel. It featured a Mexican/Chinese takeout restaurant called Wonton Pancho's, a country-western bar named Rhinestone Cowgirl, a massage parlor, three pavilions of diesel and gas pumps, free shower facilities, and an acre of parking for the big rigs.

It was dark when I parked my pickup near the fountain. I rolled both windows halfway down so that Bug would have a cross breeze and stepped outside. The gusting wind felt good against my face as I walked toward the peppermint-striped columns that flanked the motel office.

Inside the double doors, a reception area stretched fifty feet to a red-vinyl-covered front desk. The air in the low-ceilinged room reeked of industrial-strength disinfectant.

A balding man with cherub cheeks was standing behind the desk smoking the stub of a cigar. About thirty, he wore a sleeveless Syracuse basketball jersey over knee-length baggy shorts. A small plastic badge pinned to the jersey identified him as "Buntid."

"You're in luck, buddy," he said, removing the cigar as I came toward him. "We got a special today on all the rooms with a Jacuzzi."

"I've already reserved a room," I said. "The one with a view."

"You reserved a room?" he marveled, as if no one had ever done it before.

"Number ten."

"Oh, yeah," said Buntid with the light of recognition in his eyes. "The one that looks out on the diesel pumps . . . yeah . . . I saved it for you."

There was a big gap where his lower front teeth should have been. For some reason, it made him seem more sympathetic.

"Thanks," I said.

I paid him in cash for the first hour. He spread the two twenties and a ten on the countertop before stuffing them through a secure slot that connected to a lock box below. He didn't ask for my name and address, and he didn't offer me a receipt.

"You looking for a little action?" he asked, glancing toward the far end of the reception area. Near the door labeled "Restrooms" were three white vinyl couches. Five Asian women were sitting on them. They all wore loose-fitting one-piece smocks, except in different colors. Two were asleep. One was reading an Asian newspaper. They looked Korean with thick, sturdy bodies and blunt faces.

"That older one in the pink can do things with her tongue you wouldn't believe," said Buntid.

"Yeah, well, I'm expecting somebody."

The red plastic clock on the wall behind him read six forty.

"Sure," he said, picking up a metal key on a red plastic holder from the rack behind him. "I gotta tell you, if you ain't out of the room by seven thirty, it's another fifty. We rent on the hour. No partial rates. We got to change the sheets and all."

"Thanks," I said, heading for the front door.

I didn't ask him where the room was located. He had to figure I knew where it was, since I had specifically asked for it. As I went out the double doors, two elderly men were coming in.

Both in their seventies, they looked like retired Rotarians attending a Halloween party at the local senior citizen center. They wore Stetson hats and matching yellow cowboy shirts over polyester pants and geriatric walking shoes.

The first one elbowed the second and gave him a broad leer when he saw the Asian women at the end of the reception room. They headed for the vinyl couches. Welcome to the golden years.

10

Room number ten was located on the ground floor of the motel, the second to last along the left wing. Beyond the floodlit corner of the motel, I could see a line of commercial rigs parked parallel to one another across the truck stop parking lot.

I inserted the key in the door lock, stepped inside, and shut the door behind me. The room gave off the lingering smell of stale tobacco smoke and forty years of every manner of bodily excretion.

The back window looked down a refuse-littered slope to the nearest pavilion of diesel fuel tanks. An eighteen-wheeler slowed to a stop with the loud hooting of hydraulic brakes next to one of the pumps. I closed the front and back curtains and turned on the bedside floor lamp.

The room decor consisted of mirrored walls, stained indoor-outdoor carpeting, a sagging queen-sized bed, and two vinyl chairs. A fake Tiffany chandelier hung over a Formica side table.

An empty ice bucket and two plastic cups enclosed in cellophane sat on the table. There was a framed poster of a stock car driver with oversized aviator sunglasses above the headboard of the bed. The poster was bolted to the wall.

I stepped into the tiny bathroom. Another mirror hung over the cracked sink. To the left was a white plastic tub-shower enclosure screened by a red plastic curtain. I took a leak in the toilet before heading back into the bedroom.

The wind was gusting outside, but I could also hear the sounds of a woman moaning in apparent ecstasy through the wall of the room next door. The incredible adventure of it all—the theater—was the way Jordan Langford had explained it to me. It was a long way from Broadway.

I tried to visualize where the camera might have been placed during the video recording of Jordan and the girl. My eyes went to the corner of the room where the Formica table sat under the fake chandelier. The action had to have been shot from that direction. I pulled the chandelier toward me. No one seemed to have tampered with it.

Next door, the woman's moans were joined by a series of loud grunts, as if a wild boar had begun rooting for ants in the forest. Then it was quiet again except for the wind.

I knelt at the edge of the table. When I tried to move it, it wouldn't budge, and I saw that it was anchored to the floor. I slowly ran my hand down the shaft of the vertical metal stand that supported the top.

I found the convex lens of the camera about halfway down. Someone had drilled a hole the size of an M&M in the shaft before cementing the lens into position. The camera lens was facing the bed.

Using my pocket knife, I pried the transmitter out of the setting and held it up to the light. It looked like a German wireless transmitting device used by European intelligence agencies. Obsolete by current standards, it was configured to send a wireless signal to a nearby recording device.

I wondered if the rig had been set up just to record Jordan's adventures or if it was a specialty of the Wonderland. I had no way of knowing if it was still being monitored.

I unscrewed the back of the transmitter and had just removed its tiny battery when there was a soft knock on the door. Tucking the transmitter into my jeans pocket, I walked over and opened the door.

A young woman was standing in the entryway. I could hear the rustling of rain in the tree leaves behind her, beyond the parking lot. It was probably the beginning of the first rainband.

She was holding a black leather briefcase at her side. In the light of the coach lamp next to the door, I saw that her face was Eurasian. She wore a long tan raincoat that covered her slim body down to the ankles and was smiling.

The smile disappeared when she saw that I wasn't Jordan Langford.

"So sorry," she said in a lilting voice. "Wrong room."

She was much lovelier in person than she had appeared in the video, with large almond-shaped eyes and thick black hair that was exquisitely coiled around her head. She was beautiful.

"You've got the right room, Leila," I said, taking her free hand and firmly drawing her inside.

"No Leila," she protested as she came in.

"I'm Alicia's sister," I said, closing the door behind her.

There was something Central Asian about her, a definite hint of Mongol blood in the delicate half-caste face. I had seen Eurasian women with similar features in the melting pots of Jalalabad and Tashkent.

"How is the weather in Samarkand this time of year?" I asked, leaning against the closed door when she was inside.

"What? You . . . crazy . . . I want to go," she said.

She offered no resistance when I took the briefcase out of her hand, unlocked the fasteners, and spread it open. Inside the case was an assortment of lingerie; a small, powerful vibrator; several tubes of scented massage oil; and a bottle of spring water.

Wedged in the crease of one of the slatted leather dividers was the spine of a book. Letting it slide out, I saw it was a soft-cover textbook. The title was *Male Ecology: Social Development from Infancy through Adulthood*.

I glanced back at the girl. Her seemingly bewildered eyes suggested that its presence alongside the tools of her trade was one of life's great mysteries. The backflap of the book had a label that read, "Green Storm: Used Text." Green Storm was the

St. Andrews College athletic symbol. It was also the name of the college bookstore.

"Why don't you drop the pidgin English act?" I said, still blocking the door. "It needs work."

"Pliss," she said, her eyes darting to the window and then back to me. "I want to go," she repeated.

Considering there was no public transportation within twenty miles, I went through the rest of the briefcase looking for her driver's license. Aside from an assortment of ribbed condoms and three fifty-dollar bills, there was nothing else inside it. She had probably left her purse and identification in the car. Replacing the book and her money, I closed the briefcase and refastened the locks.

"So how did you get into blackmail, Leila?" I asked, handing it back to her.

"Just pleasure girl," she said in the same singsong voice.

"I'm an undercover police officer," I came back with a ferocious stare, hauling out my wallet and flashing my cheesy campus security badge. "You can drop this act and talk to me here, or I'll arrest you now and take you down to headquarters."

I had always wanted to use a line like that.

"I would never attempt to blackmail President Langford," she replied in Oxford-accented English.

It was my turn to be impressed.

"How did you know who he was?" I demanded.

"I'm a junior at St. Andrews," she said. "I recognized him as soon as he came to meet me the first time."

"What's your real name?"

"Miram Shakirov."

"Where are you from?"

"Uzbekistan. Tashkent. I'm here on a full government scholarship."

I held out one of the vinyl chairs for her. She opened the buttons of her raincoat before sitting. Her low-cut silk blouse displayed unusual cleavage for an Uzbek woman.

"Are you half Russian?" I asked her in Uzbek Arabic.

Her eyes widened in surprise for a moment before she nodded.

"What kind of policeman are you?" she asked.

"I handle all the Uzbek cases in the New York Finger Lakes," I said. "So why did you use the fake accent, Miram?"

"I . . . didn't want him to be embarrassed," she answered. "I think he's an amazing man."

"Right," I said. "You think he's amazing. So when did you decide to let the blackmailers know who he was?"

"What blackmailers? I didn't . . . I never told anyone."

"Come on, Miram. We both know blackmail pays a lot better than selling yourself."

"I'm not selling myself," she said hotly. "I do this because I'm studying to go into the hospitality industry."

"The hospitality industry," I repeated.

"I'm raising the seed capital to create a franchised network of legalized sexual service centers," she said. "My company is called Please Release Me. You can learn all about it on my website."

When I continued to stare at her skeptically, she said, "It's true . . . I've already received contingent commitment letters from two venture capital firms that have read my business plan."

The story sounded too ridiculous to believe she was making it all up. The way the world was going, she would probably make a fortune with it. But that didn't mean she hadn't also figured out a way to make Jordan pay a share of her capitalization costs.

"Did you ever see anyone else when you were with him in this room?" I asked. "Someone who might have planted a camera to record what you were doing here?"

Her eyes seemed shocked.

"No," she said firmly. "Never."

Checking my watch, I saw that it was already seven twenty. Not wanting to shell out another fifty dollars, I decided to walk her back to her car to check her identification and ask about the call-girl service. Maybe she had passed along Jordan's identity to someone working there.

"All right, let's go," I said, standing up.

From the look on her face, I saw that she thought I was arresting her.

"Now that we are both here," she said, looking up at me with those lovely almond eyes, "might I possibly please you in some way?"

It's funny, getting older. Your knees might be swollen with arthritis and there might be enough crow's feet around your eyes to inspire Edgar Allan Poe, but part of you wants to believe you've still got it. The old magic.

"You're a very good-looking man," she said, her eyes posed invitingly.

"Yeah," I said, grinning back. I could imagine her saying exactly the same thing to the two senior citizen cowboys I had seen in the reception area.

"No . . . you are," she insisted as I tried to remember the name of the call-girl service she worked with. Friends with All the Benefits . . . that was the name the woman used when I had called to set up the appointment. The girl had to know where they were located, and I doubted it was very far away. That would be my next stop. I decided to take her with me.

"Please don't arrest me," she said, her voice going soft.

"Not if you cooperate, Miram."

I was about to ask her the address of Friends with All the Benefits when there was another knock at the door. She appeared startled at the interruption as I went to open it, expecting Buntid to be there, looking for his next fifty and asking how I was enjoying the view.

A man in a flowered Hawaiian shirt was standing in the sheltered walkway that connected the ground-floor rooms. Behind him, the sky was filled with rain. I could hear its steady rapping on the slanted roof.

"So who are you, man?" he asked with a cocky grin.

He was in his late twenties, short and stocky, with simian arms that nearly reached his knees. His body-builder's physique was undercut a little by an almost girlish pretty face. He had long dark eyelashes and a button nose. His thick brown hair was tied off in a ponytail.

"You don't know?" I came back.

"I know you got something of mine," he said.

In the faint gleam of the headlights passing by on the thruway, I saw a hint of movement in the darkness behind him and realized he wasn't alone. The second man was standing out in the rain beyond the sheltered walkway.

"I paid for this fabulous room," I said. "You can both have it when I'm finished."

"You got something that belongs to me," he repeated, no longer grinning. "I want it."

"Really? What's that?" I asked.

"You know what it is. We saw you take it."

"So you're the movie maker . . . you need the camera to go to Hollywood, right?"

"Keep it up, wiseass," he said.

"I think I'll just hold onto it until I find out why you put it there, Beauty."

"What did you say, asshole?"

His right hand slowly dipped into the hip pocket of his pants.

I could feel my heart pumping against my chest and took a deep breath. In my mind's eye, I saw the Colt .45 tucked in its hiding place next to the chimney in the cabin and silently cursed myself.

"You're as pretty as a girl," I said. "But I guess all the guys tell you that."

His right hand swung back into the light holding a butter-fly knife. With a flick of his wrist, the flashing blade whipped toward me.

"You can get hurt with one of those, Beauty."

As I slipped my hand into my jeans pocket, I remembered that I had left my own knife on the table inside the room. Instead, I found the few coins I had taken in change after buying the sandwich and coffee.

"You'll find out soon enough, asshole," he said, taking a step toward the open doorway.

Big Jim Dickey had told me I was going to seed, and he was probably right. I wondered whether I still had anything left as he bent forward into a low wrestler's stance and moved toward me, the knife extended in his right hand.

Beyond the walkway, I heard the light crunch of the other man's shoes on the gravel parking lot as he headed toward the room. A moment later, the coach lamp that illuminated the doorway went out.

"Stay out of it, Angie . . . this prick's mine," said Beauty.

"Angie?" I asked. "You brought your girlfriend along to help?"

"I'm gonna cut your balls off," he rasped.

He moved slowly toward me, keeping his left foot in front of the right just as I would have done. When he was three feet away, he feinted to the right and then lunged at me, thrusting the blade in a short upward arc and slitting the loose fold of my shirt as I stepped back and to the side.

I felt a sharp sting and then a warm stream of blood running down my chest. Palming the coins from my pocket in my right hand, I backed across the motel room. With his apelike arms, his reach was well beyond mine.

As he closed the distance again, I hurled the coins into his face and launched a kick with my right boot that caught his hand in midswing. The butterfly knife flew across the room.

Hearing sudden movement behind me, I remembered that Leila was still there and could be part of their action. Turning quickly, I saw she had pried open the back window. Already half-through, she looked back at me with terror-stricken eyes.

For a body builder, Beauty moved fast. A moment later, he was riding my back, his left elbow cutting off the air to my windpipe and the fingers of his right hand clawing for my eyes. When I tried to throw him off, he wrapped his legs around my thighs.

Knowing that the other man was still out there, I lugged him close enough to kick the door shut. It was the type that locked automatically. Two seconds later, a body slammed into it.

Angie wasn't his girlfriend or kid sister. Thankfully, the door held.

Shielding my eyes with my right hand, I swung around in a full circle and then drove Beauty into the nearest wall, smashing the plate glass mirror. It didn't loosen his hold. While I struggled to breathe, he kept clawing at me with his fingernails, his head just behind mine, his gnashing teeth trying to reach my left ear.

I was able to reach the side of his jaw with my right hand. Curling my index and middle finger into the rigid shape of a fishhook, I thrust them inside his cheek and ripped at his mouth with all my strength.

"Angie!" he screamed as the corner of his mouth split open and tore along the jawline.

In response, there was another booming slam against the door. It began to splinter as Beauty's legs came free from my thighs. Pulling my fingers loose from his ruined mouth, I dipped my shoulder to the left and heaved him across my back. He landed on the bed and was back on his feet a moment later.

He was trying to scrabble back into a wrestler's clinch when I grabbed his left wrist, levered his arm over my knee, and snapped it downward, dislocating his elbow.

He screamed again as the door shattered behind us. I chopped down hard on the back of Beauty's neck and the screaming stopped.

As the second man came through the door, I saw that he was close to my own height but twenty pounds heavier. Maybe forty-five years old, he was wearing a sleeveless tank top that revealed a blacksmith's arms and big knobby hands. His left eye was milky white.

He came toward me in a fighter's crouch, both fists protecting his face above the slab of his chest. From the flattened nose and scar tissue around his eyes, he had probably been a professional, but not a very good one. Moving counterclockwise, I began throwing quick jabs at his head to keep him away from me, hoping to throw a straight right as soon as he dropped his hands.

Blood was still running into my eyes from one of the gouges Beauty had carved in me. The guy ducked left and threw a solid hook that caught me on the temple, backing me toward the front window. Quickly following up, he threw a straight left with most of his weight behind it. The punch landed flush on my jaw, and I went down hard, instinctively rolling over as the toe of his boot glanced off my upper thigh.

It was Beauty who saved me, choosing that moment to try to shove himself up from the floor. As the old fighter stepped back to launch a kick at my groin, he tripped over Beauty, going down to one knee.

Even as I scrambled to my feet, I knew I had to end it or they would soon be filleting me with the butterfly knife. The big guy was smiling as he came on, sensing I was almost done. Flicking a hard jab in my face, he followed it with a left-right combination, driving me back toward the Formica table. I grabbed the chandelier to stay on my feet, and it swung me around far enough that his next roundhouse punch missed me completely. As he lunged past, I delivered a solid right hook to his Adam's apple.

His good eye went blank for a moment, and he stumbled before turning to come back at me. He was moving slower now and having trouble breathing. Pivoting around to his blind side, I drove a hard punch to his kidneys, and he grunted out loud. It was the first noise he had made since battering his way into the room. He swung back wildly at me, but the punch missed as I ducked away.

Head down, he charged me, and I kicked him in the right knee. As he buckled toward me, I straightened him with an uppercut to the jaw, feeling the shock of it all the way up my shoulder. He reeled back several feet before dropping heavily to the floor. He was struggling to get up again when I kicked him in the head and he lay still.

For several seconds I stood there swaying back and forth, my left shoulder numb, both legs trembling. I felt a wave of gray nausea, but at least my head was still on my shoulders. That was a start. Glancing across the room, I saw that Beauty was trying to crawl across the floor. He was advancing a few inches at a time, whimpering softly as he tried to cradle the dislocated elbow in his right hand.

The splintered motel room door swung open, and I looked up to see a woman standing in the shattered doorframe. It was one of the Korean women from the reception area.

She was holding a fresh set of towels and two clean sheets in her arms. Apparently she did double duty on the maid staff. Her fathomless black eyes took in the wreckage of the room without any noticeable reaction.

"We're still tidying up here . . . just a few more minutes," I said, attempting to smile.

11

I went into the bathroom and soaked a towel in hot water. After washing the blood off my face, I broke a cardinal rule and glanced in the mirror. It wasn't as bad as I thought.

There were raw cuts and scratches around both eyes. I had a fairly deep gouge beneath the right one that was seeping blood. Beauty hadn't succeeded in getting his fingernails into either eye.

Aside from the scratches, the left side of my jaw was swelling, and I could move one of my front teeth with my index finger. Lifting the lower edge of my bloody polo shirt, I saw that the cut on my chest was superficial. Rinsing the towel in hot water, I went back into the room.

Beauty was still inching along the floor on his quest to get to the doorway. Picking up one of the vinyl chairs, I trudged past him and shut the splintered door as far as I could, wedging the back of the chair against the knob to keep it closed against the wind and rain.

Gripping the back of his collar, I dragged him over to the other chair and sat down. Turning him over on his back, I gently wiped the bloody slime away from his mouth.

"You're going to need stitches, Beauty," I said. "But you'll be as pretty as ever in a month or two."

An odd whistling sound came from his torn mouth before he managed to snarl, "Fr . . . fr . . . frock . . . you."

I turned him over to the side to search his pockets. The first one yielded a pair of engraved brass knuckles. They were studded with sharpened conical points that extended a half inch from the frame.

"You get these in your Christmas stocking?" I asked.

In his back pocket, I found a key to room fourteen at the Wonderland and a black leather wallet.

"Goin' . . . kill you," he snarled into the chair leg as I rolled him over on his back again.

He had five hundred dollars in fifties and twenties, along with two credit cards and a business card that read, "Devane Investigations Unlimited," with a Syracuse mailing address. The wallet also contained a faded two-inch-square photograph of a naked blonde girl with enormous breasts. She was staring bleakly into the camera and looked to be about fifteen.

The driver's license identified him as Salvatore Scalise, 16 Windsor Court, Liverpool, New York. I seemed to remember Liverpool being near Syracuse, which was about sixty miles back down the thruway.

"Listen, Sal . . . we don't have a lot of time here," I said, expecting to hear sirens any minute and not wanting to spend the rest of the night filling out police reports. "I need to know who you work for. It's important."

"Frock . . . you . . . bastid," he said.

I knew I could track the girl down pretty quickly. There couldn't be too many juniors at St. Andrews from Uzbekistan. But I doubted I would find her in her dorm room or sorority when I got back to Groton.

She would almost certainly go to ground for the rest of the weekend, if not longer, and Jordan was facing the blackmailer's deadline. That left Sal as my only lead to who was blackmailing Jordan and had possibly murdered Dennis Wheatley.

"Sal . . . I don't want to hurt you," I said. "Tell me who you work for and we can both be on our way."

He raised his head off the floor and tried to spit at me, but only ended up with bloody drool on his ruined mouth. Reaching down, I slowly pulled his dislocated elbow toward me. When he screamed out again, I covered his mouth.

"I really don't want to do this, Sal," I said and meant it. "Now, is taping the customers one of your regular duties here at the Wonderland or were you hired just to film the man who was supposed to be in this room tonight?"

I took my hand away from his mouth.

"Goin' kill you, man . . . frist chance," was his next answer. The eyes looking up at me were snake-hard.

Lifting his dislocated arm, I dug my boot into his armpit and pinioned his wrist with my left hand. With my right, I bent his pinky finger back until it was nearly ready to snap.

As soon as the scream subsided, he threw up on himself.

"Now I'll ask you once more. Do you do this for the Wonderland or were you hired to film just the man in this room?"

He slowly shook his head back and forth, his eyes closed.

"You've got guts, Sal, but if you don't tell me what I need to know, I'll have to snap this finger like a lobster claw. Then we'll have only nine more to go," I said.

I never would have done it, but after digesting that thought for several seconds, he grunted, "Jess the nigger. Only the nigger."

"And how did you know the man was going to be here?" I demanded, continuing the pressure on his finger.

"Don't know . . . we was told to be here at six and set up the camera like we done before."

"Who told you?"

He shook his head back and forth.

"Who told you?" I repeated, bending the same finger back to the breaking point.

"Bobby Devane!" he shouted up at me from the floor.

"Doesn't help me . . . I don't know him," I said, not letting up on the pressure.

"Oh, God, man . . . he works for the Razzano brothers," he cried, the words coming now in a rush.

"Who are they?"

"Lawyers . . . the guys on TV."

"As in, 'If you've swallowed asbestos, call us'?" I asked.

When he nodded, I eased up on his finger again and he drew in a long breath. Even I had heard of the Razzano brothers. Their two conniving faces were plastered everywhere from roadside billboards to the back cover of the Groton telephone book. Theirs was the law firm that had agreed to represent Kelly in her age discrimination lawsuit against Hustlers.

"Where can I find Bobby Devane?" I asked, getting up from the bed.

"Devane . . . Investigashons," he said, struggling to pronounce the second word. "Shiracuse."

I took the business card out of Sal's wallet. There was a cell phone number for Devane that someone had handwritten on the back of the card. I dropped the wallet and his money on the floor next to him. As I was heading for the door, the house phone began ringing and I picked it up. It was Buntid calling from the front desk.

"Maid came back and said you was still in the room," he said firmly. "That's another fifty bucks like I told you."

Apparently, she hadn't told him the condition of the room. It was probably because she didn't speak anything but Korean and the other, more universal language. It also struck me that maybe the Wonderland was used to this kind of stuff. I looked over at Angie. He was still out cold on the floor. Sal was trying for the door again, like a baby turtle in the Galapagos yearning to reach the sea.

"Yeah, I've got guests here that might want to stay awhile. You probably want to send someone down to collect it."

"I'm on my way," he said.

I removed the chair from the back of the door and swung it open.

"Goin' to kill you, man . . . frist chance," honked Sal from the floor as I walked out of the room.

12

The rain had stopped as I made my way down to room fourteen. Inside, I found Sal's recording equipment along with a large metal case stuffed with several thousand dollars' worth of surveillance toys. In a separate zipped compartment, I found two more video recordings in plastic sleeves. I took it all with me and stowed everything in the tool compartment behind the cab of the pickup.

As soon as Bug smelled the blood on me, she began whimpering. It took me a minute to quiet her down as we headed back toward Groton. Still feeling like someone had tried to split my skull with an ax blade, I rummaged in the glove compartment and came up with a bottle of Ibuprofen. I dry swallowed four of them.

The deeper cuts were continuing to seep blood, and I stopped at the same Quik Mart where I had bought a sandwich on the way up. While I was paying for Band Aids and another twenty ounces of coffee, the woman behind the counter noticed my torn and bloody polo shirt. When her eyes drifted upward, she stared at my face as if trying to match it to a wanted poster.

Another rain squall began drubbing the windshield as I got on the road again. While driving back, I replayed the encounter at the Wonderland over and over in my mind.

You stupid asshole, I thought. At Ranger school, I had been trained to dismantle idiots like Sal and Angie without working up a sweat. I could imagine my old training instructor, First Sergeant Jim Bombard, looking over my shoulder during the brawl at the motel room.

"You're fightin' like a goddamn cherry, Cantrell," he would have shouted at me.

And he would have been right. Maybe it was a good thing, I decided. This wasn't Afghanistan, and they weren't my country's enemies. They were only two scum-balls who worked for blackmailers.

I tried to concentrate on what it all meant.

Someone had hired a private detective named Bobby Devane to spy on Jordan. The request could have come from the Razzano law firm, or it might have been a freelance job. Either way, I had to find out, and very soon.

Whoever had hired Devane also knew exactly when Jordan was going to be at the Wonderland, with enough advance notice to send Sal there to set up the surveillance equipment. That information could only have come indirectly from Jordan himself or from the call-girl service. Jordan had told me in his office that he had made some enemies, but he hadn't said who they were.

It was a little past nine when I arrived back home. The wet spruce trees around the cabin were glistening in the headlights as I pulled up to the back door. Turning off the engine, I saw that the windows were dark.

I thought I had left a light on in the living room. It was possible that the storm had knocked out the electricity. Switching the headlights back on, I walked to the cabin door. Bug stayed by my side. After turning the knob, I swung the door open and waited. Bug stepped over the threshold, stopped, and sniffed the air. She turned her head to look back up at me with a bemused expression that said everything was fine.

I went to the table lamp in the living room and discovered that the bulb had burned out. I wondered whether I was losing my nerve as I went to turn off the truck lights.

Inside, I went to the bathroom and took a quick glance in the mirror. My face looked worse. Thankfully, the Ibuprofen had blunted my headache. Using my index finger, I tried to move my front lower tooth again. I hoped I wouldn't lose it.

The knuckles on both hands were a more immediate problem. The three on the right were in bad shape, the middle finger already swollen. If I didn't ice them right away, they would be almost useless for a day or two.

I was soaking both hands in a bowl of ice in the kitchen sink when I saw headlights filtering through the trees from the lake road, and a car came slowly down the driveway in the rain. I turned off the kitchen light and waited by the window.

It was Jordan's ten-year-old Volvo. I dried my hands and headed for the front door. As usual, his timing was perfect. The visit would give me the chance to ask him all the questions I had come up with on the ride back from the Wonderland.

Only it wasn't Jordan.

"Happy birthday," said Blair from the shadows.

I had forgotten that my birthday was coming up in a few days. I was even more surprised that she remembered the date.

"Thanks," I said.

There was an awkward silence. I wondered how she knew where I lived.

"I'm sorry to come here like this," she said, "but I need to talk to you, Jake."

She didn't wait for an invitation to come in, walking past me through the dark entrance into the living room as if we were still living together and she had just gotten back to our apartment after class.

Taking off her wet raincoat, she hung it on a peg by the fireplace. She was wearing a blue nylon warm-up suit and sneakers. Her hair was fixed in a ponytail. Bug came over and stood by my side as she turned toward me. When she saw my face in the light, her eyes widened in alarm.

"What happened to you?"

"Just some new character lines," I said.

"Tell me the truth, goddamn it," she demanded, her face pale.

"I was in a fight."

There was no point in lying to her. The results were self-evident as she came toward me. She looked down and saw the swollen knuckles.

"Jesus, Jake," she said. "Do you have any antiseptic?"

She followed me through the kitchen and into the bathroom.

"In the medicine chest," I said.

She found some Merthiolate and cotton balls along with a bottle of hydrogen peroxide. While I sat on the closed toilet seat, she leaned over me and began to clean the abrasions on my face.

"Just like old times," she said with a laugh, "with me here to bind your wounds."

That familiar laugh. It seemed to well up from deep inside her.

"Those were football games," I said.

I felt her breath on my cheek as she cleaned and patched. Her fingers moved across my face with agile dexterity.

"This is going to sting a bit," she said, holding the cotton ball soaked in Merthiolate against the deep gouge under my right eye.

It did.

"Do you know why I fell for you?" she said, her lips just a few inches away.

"Ancient history," I said.

What was it that made her so compelling? She was beautiful, but it wasn't a classic beauty. Maybe it was her eyes. They were a chameleon's eyes, a startling violet with little gold flecks in the iris that came alive whenever she got excited.

"That first night we met . . . one of my girlfriends pointed you out across the room," she said with a chuckle in her throat. "'What a magnificent animal,' she said to me. And it was true, Jake. You looked so indestructible back then. You had that incredible hardness about you . . . your face, your shoulders, your legs . . . every part of you."

"Yeah, I was a Greek god."

She reacted to my sarcasm with a stern elevation of one brow.

"But that wasn't why I fell for you," she continued, the gold flecks now lighting up. "When we were introduced, I fully expected you to give me some stupid jock line that would lead right back to your bedroom."

I remembered that night.

"And the first thing you wanted to discuss that night was Hemingway versus Fitzgerald . . . which one was the greater writer," she went on.

"Which one was it?"

"Fitzgerald . . . you thought he was the best writer of the century . . . and then I saw that your eyes weren't hard at all . . . and then when you smiled . . . God you were beautiful, Jake."

And Jordan was more beautiful. And he cared enough about her dreams of changing the world to do something about it.

I didn't respond to the compliment.

"All better now?" she asked softly.

Her face was still inches from mine, the familiar soapy scent of her all around me when she leaned down and kissed my mouth. It was a sweet kiss, nothing more, just a gentle brushing of her lips. She pulled her face back and smiled.

"I read once that a kiss was designed by God or nature to stop speech when words become superfluous," she said.

"Why are you here, Blair?" I asked, breaking the mood.

Her smile slowly evaporated. When she turned to put away the Merthiolate, I stood up and went out to the kitchen. She followed me.

"Do you have a drink?" she asked.

I had to laugh. In the years since she had left, I had probably consumed a small warehouse full of them.

"Sure," I said, pouring myself one from the open bottle of Johnnie Walker.

Glancing over my shoulder, she spied a split of Hennessy's that was sitting on the shelf over the sink. I had lifted it from the banquet table after a St. Andrews faculty benefit in support of efforts to establish contact with "otherworld benevolent beings."

Blair opened the split, poured it into a coffee mug, and added two ice cubes from the bowl in which I had been soaking my hands.

"There's something wrong with Jordan," she said, her low voice barely audible over the wind and rain buffeting the windows.

Yeah, I thought. *Your husband dresses up like a lingerie model a couple times a month. That might be part of the problem.*

"I think he might be having a nervous breakdown."

I remained silent, wondering how much she knew.

"He refuses to tell me what it is, but he has been acting strangely, going out at all hours. Now he's even sleeping in the den. Two nights ago, I went down there and . . ."

Tears swelled over her lower eyelids and slowly ran down her cheeks. It seemed like a good moment to take her into my arms and comfort her the way an old lover should always be ready to do. Instead, I stepped away from her.

"Jake . . . he was sobbing," she said.

Lifting the mug to her mouth, she knocked the Hennessy down in one long swallow. I heard the ice cubes clink against her teeth.

"So . . . why me?" I asked.

"Because his secretary told me that you saw him this morning. You must know something, Jake. Please tell me what's going on. I can't help him unless I know what it is."

I debated whether to tell her what was happening.

"I love him, Jake," she said. "You know that more than anyone."

I felt the familiar anger welling inside me and barely managed to control it. She must have seen it in my battered face.

"God knows . . . you deserve a better explanation for what happened back then, Jake."

Taking my hand, she led me over to the couch in front of the fireplace.

"When I first went out to join Jordan, it was simply for the job . . . you have to believe that. I was still in love with you then, and terribly worried about what might happen to you in Afghanistan. But I was also turning against the war . . . all war."

She waited for me to say something. I didn't.

"I had no idea what it would be like in Detroit, but from the first day I started my job, it was just . . . pure adrenaline . . . like I was plugged into some powerful electrical current . . . a force that could truly empower people and change their lives. It was Jordan, really, at least at the start. He had grown so much since I had known him in college. He was so poised . . . so charismatic."

Her face had taken on that inner glow I remembered, reflecting the light.

"We were working out of a decrepit storefront in one of the worst neighborhoods in the city. But people were coming there for help. And he was showing those powerless people how to take control of their lives, giving them the tools they needed to solve the problems they confronted every day in the streets . . . the homelessness, the drugs, the violence. When they realized he wasn't out for himself, they began to believe in him; he started getting real support."

"When did your feelings for him change?"

She smiled at me. It was a sad smile.

"I guess it started with a sense of admiration for what he was accomplishing with his life. After Yale, he could have gone into the most prestigious law firms in the country . . . but he chose to be there. As the operation grew, he began treating me as a full partner, knowing he could rely on me to do things well. After a few months, we were doing everything together . . . it evolved, you see. I never wanted to hurt you, Jake. But when he told me he loved me, I . . . I just knew it was right . . . I was part of his life and his work, and I wanted to be."

"And now?" I asked.

"And now . . . it isn't the same. Back then, we were making a true difference in people's lives, and we were doing it together, wherever the work took us, partners in every sense. Here at St. Andrews, I feel like a politician's wife. My job is to entertain faculty wives, cut ribbons on new building projects, and stand by his side while he strokes the big givers who just want their name on things . . . I hate it here."

"Life is tough," I said.

"We've talked about going back to Detroit," she said. "That's what I'm hoping for."

The conversation hadn't answered any of my more pressing questions.

"Does Jordan have any enemies?" I asked her.

"Enemies?" she asked, taking ten seconds to think about it. "There are people here who don't like him. There have always been people who don't like the idea of us as a couple if that's what you mean."

"That's it?"

"I think so. Why?"

"What about Dennis Wheatley?"

Shaking her head, she said, "Dennis worshipped him." A moment later, she added, "Does his death have something to do with this?"

"Have you received any threatening notes in recent weeks?"

"No. At least I'm not aware of any," she said, her face going pale again. "What's going on, Jake?"

A sudden gust of wind blew open the porch door. It slammed against the inside wall with a loud bang, and she visibly started at the noise. Across the lake, a bolt of lightning arced across the black sky.

"What's going on, Jake?" she repeated.

"I'm not sure," I said. "I'm trying to find out."

"Then just tell me what you know."

"Why don't you ask Jordan?"

"I already have, but he won't tell me anything."

"That's his decision then," I said. "Look, Blair, I'm really tired. I've got to get a few hours of sleep."

Her eyes clouded with anger.

"You're pathetic," she said.

"You're right."

Without another word, she took her raincoat off the peg by the fireplace. I heard the front door slam and the Volvo start up. From the kitchen window, I watched the car move off through the swaying spruce trees until the lights disappeared.

You stupid asshole, I thought. It was only after she was gone that I realized she had never bothered to ask me why I had gotten into a fight. Picking up the phone, I entered Jordan's cell number. After five rings, I got his voice mail recording. I left a message for him to call me as soon as he could and hung up.

Going over to the kitchen counter, I poured myself another Johnnie Walker.

"Happy birthday," I said aloud to myself.

As a kid, before my parents died, the day had seemed important. Would I finally get the .410 shotgun? The cat boat? Of course I would. It was my birthday, the most important day in the whole world.

The world had shrunk a lot since. For now, there was just Bug and me.

Heading back into my bedroom, I lay down on the bed. Bug joined me there a few seconds later, crawling slowly up onto her side of the coverlet. I decided to close my eyes for a few minutes, figuring that Jordan would be calling back soon.

I dreamed of Afghanistan.

13

"It could be a trap, Major," he called out to me in the dream, just as he had called out those same words on that bitterly cold night near Kandahar.

"It probably is a trap, Sergeant," I told him as we waited in the darkness of the bombed-out village.

The S-2 in our battalion's intelligence shop had convinced the colonel that one of the border chieftains in our sector was willing to bring two important Taliban leaders over to our side.

My special operations team was ordered to secure the ground for an Afghan army escort that would meet them in a small village near Lashkar Gah and then take them on to Kandahar.

We infiltrated the village shortly after night fell and found it deserted. I assigned three of my men to wait inside the only building still standing for the arrival of the Taliban leaders. The rest of us took up positions behind the stone walls that surrounded the village. I made sure we had a full field of fire for our M249 Squad Automatic Weapons in case it was a trap.

A few minutes after the scheduled rendezvous time, a small caravan of vehicles rolled into the village. Through my infrared scope, I saw that they were driving Afghan army trucks.

The men who emerged from the vehicles were dressed in American camouflage uniforms. There were ten of them, and they were equipped with American-supplied M-4 carbines and MP-5 submachine guns, just like us.

Half of them went inside the building. I radioed my unit commander to tell him that the Taliban group still hadn't gotten there but that the escort had just arrived. He said that was impossible because the Afghan army escort had been delayed by a car bombing in Kandahar. That's when I knew we had been betrayed. They were Taliban fighters, and we were their target.

I ordered my team to open fire. A few moments later, the Taliban who had entered the building burst out through the door. They were cut down before they reached their vehicles. The Taliban fighters who had been deployed outside disappeared into the darkness.

We found the three men in my combat team inside the building. They had paid with their lives for my mistake. Each one of them had been horribly mutilated before he died.

In my dream, the three of them stood before me again, their knife-punctured eyes pleading for me to save them. I was wrenched out of the nightmare by the jarring ring of the telephone.

My jaw felt as if someone was boring into it with a dull bit. The muscles in my shoulders and back were aching. Lying across the bed, Bug was giving me a vicious glare that suggested enough was enough with these late-night disturbances.

I remembered leaving the message for Jordan to call me back as soon as possible. Swinging my knees over the edge of the bed, I stood up. Once on my feet, the forward motion took my legs into the kitchen, where I picked up the phone. Whoever was calling hung up just as I got there. I heard only a dial tone.

"Shit," I said.

Looking at the wall clock, I saw that it was three thirty. The storm had risen in intensity since I had gone to sleep.

I went into the bathroom. Searching under the sink, I found a dust-covered bottle of Listerine. After rinsing out my mouth, I tried to move the loosened tooth again. It might have been my imagination, but it seemed a little tighter. I was taking some satisfaction in that when the phone began ringing again.

"Officer Cantrell?" asked the voice almost timidly.

"Yes, Carlene," I replied.

"You're needed here right away," she said.

"Maybe you don't know it, Carlene, but I'm officially suspended from duty," I said. "I'm only a liaison."

"I know that," she came right back, "but Captain Morgo asked me to call you to please come right away."

I wasn't about to have any part of it.

"Sorry, but I'm waiting for an important call."

There was another short pause before she blurted, "We have another deceased individual on campus. The caller said the dead man is hanging from the suspension footbridge."

For a moment I wondered if I might be traveling through a time warp.

"Didn't we have this conversation last night?" I asked.

"Yes," she said. "But . . . this is a new one . . . Captain Morgo is on her way there now. She asked me to find you as soon as possible. She told me to tell you—"

Her voice was cut off midsentence. I heard a gurgle in the phone line and it went dead. I wasn't surprised. My telephone line ran along the forest road, and it took just one falling limb to wipe out service for everyone farther down the lake.

Putting down the phone, I stepped out onto the front porch. The temperature had dropped at least ten degrees, and the wind was probably gusting at forty miles an hour. I turned on the floodlight that was mounted on the end of the cabin roof. In its glare, I could see that the rain was being driven almost horizontally by the wind.

A hundred feet out, the surface of the lake looked like the North Atlantic. White-capped waves were slamming into the shoreline, sweeping right over the dock pilings and up the grassy rise toward the cabin. The base of the apple tree next to the dock was already underwater. My old heavy bag was swinging back and forth as if stuffed with feathers.

I heard a ripping sound followed by a loud resounding crack. As I watched, an eighty-foot-high spruce tree came roaring down, smashing straight through the roof of the neighbor's art studio in the next compound.

I bolted the porch door behind me and headed back into the bedroom. After putting on a denim work shirt, boxer shorts, and white athletic socks, I went to the hiding place next to the chimney and strapped on my leather shoulder harness, socketing the .45 automatic into its holster.

After snugging the chest strap, I put on my army-issue waterproofs along with rubber wading boots. Loading two spare magazines with ammunition, I secured them in the side pocket of my jacket. The last thing I did before leaving the cabin was make sure Bug had plenty of water in her bowl. There wasn't time to make her breakfast.

I could see she wasn't thrilled about being left inside the cabin with no access to the porch or the lawn, but I didn't have time to explain it to her before locking the door behind me.

The pickup was rocking in the wind when I started it up and began heading toward Groton. The road surface was already littered with downed branches and wind-driven debris. I kept my speed down to thirty so I had time to swerve around the bigger obstacles.

About a mile from town, several deer ran wildly across the road past my headlights. Although I braked right away, it was impossible to avoid hitting the last one with a glancing fender blow.

A hefty buck, he skidded across the gravel road for ten yards, rolled over, and came up on his feet. As I watched, he shook himself and trotted off after the others.

"You and me both, brother," I called out to him as I drove on.

Heading up the steep grade along the gorge, I saw that the lower windows of the Fall Creek Tavern were lit up like an ocean liner. As I passed by, people were standing three deep at the bar, confirming the old axiom that storms bring people together. Of course, for the regulars, any reason to drink was a good reason.

I pulled into the overlook parking lot next to the suspension footbridge. Captain Morgo's police cruiser was already there, its lights out. There was no indication that I was approaching a crime scene.

Taking my flashlight and work gloves, I headed down the path toward the bridge. Through the driving rain, I could see a dark figure standing under the trees. Ken Macready emerged out of the downpour, his uniform covered by a wildly flapping green poncho. He trained his flashlight on my face as I came toward him.

"What the . . . ?" he began.

"I ran into some barbed wire," I said. "So what happened here?"

"We've got another dead guy," he said, coming to attention. "He's right in the same place as the one yesterday."

"Where's Captain Morgo?" I asked loudly.

He pointed toward the bridge. "She's already out there."

"What about the sheriff?"

"They've already had three storm-related deaths . . . He radioed the captain a few minutes ago that he would get here as soon as he could."

"Any word on when the storm is going to peak?"

"According to the weather service, we won't see the worst of it until later this morning. Right now it's gusting about forty-five."

A purple-white flash of lightning lit up the dark sky, followed by a crash of thunder.

"What's the hurricane's name again?" I asked with a reassuring grin.

"Ilse."

"Yeah," I said. "Just a little pussy cat . . . nothing to worry about."

His young freckled face grinned back at me.

"Let's get to work," I said.

Together we continued down the path toward the bridge.

Remembering Carlene's words about there being another caller, I stopped at the blue-light emergency phone. I opened the door of the metal housing with the tip of my finger and shined my flashlight in. There was only bare wire again. The new phone was gone like the last one.

"Just like last time," said Ken.

Under the college's service contract, our electronic security provider was responsible for repairing the emergency phones within an hour of a reported outage. Assuming they had done so, the killer was for some reason following the same pattern. It could only be because he wanted us to know it was him.

"What did you do with that camcorder footage you took of everyone who was here yesterday?"

"Captain Morgo gave the camera back to the guy. But I've got the recorded material in my desk at the office."

"Good man," I said. "We'll watch it later."

I pulled up the hood of my waterproof jacket to keep the rain out of my eyes and to hide the damage to my face from Captain Morgo. She would probably find it another docking offense.

"Don't let anyone out there except the sheriff's men," I said, leaving him at the entrance.

On the suspension bridge, the gusting blasts of wind drowned out the cataract of wild water racing down the gorge two hundred feet below me. The reinforced concrete path of the bridge was swaying under my feet as I approached the shadowy outline of Captain Morgo. She was standing halfway across the span and gripping the bridge railing with both hands.

Her skin was the color of a ripe avocado. The force of the wind gusts was inflating her cheeks, puffing them up like a squirrel gathering nuts for the winter. Uneasily taking one hand off the railing to face me, she looked up and shouted, "I . . . need your help."

As she raised her head, the wind flipped her uniform hat off her head, and it went sailing over the rail behind her. I could see the open terror in her eyes. Even with the Glock 17 on her hip, she looked like nothing so much as a bedraggled grandmother in a gaudy police uniform, vulnerable and defenseless. When another gust shook the bridge, she grabbed the railing again with both hands.

"These are designed to take a lot worse than this," I shouted to her.

Taking a guarded step toward me, she took my left hand in hers and grasped it hard. Putting her mouth closer to my ear, she shouted, "I was wrong about all this, Jake."

Looking down at her, my past anger just melted away.

I nodded once and squeezed her hand in return.

"Do you know who it is yet?" I shouted over the wind.

She shook her head and yelled, "The call came in less than twenty minutes ago. I just got here."

I trained my flashlight on the walkway beside her. It looked almost exactly like the scene I had encountered the previous night. The end of the brightly colored rope was lashed around the railing with the same stopper hitch. Sitting in the lee of the wind at the foot of the railing was a green plastic drinking cup.

The intricately braided cord looked identical to the other one, with the end knot shaped like a golden acorn. The cord even appeared to be lashed in exactly the same place on the bridge. I leaned out over the railing and trained the flashlight down at the swaying corpse.

"Be careful," cried Captain Morgo as she grabbed the bottom edge of my waterproof jacket in her powerful hands.

There was an important difference between this death scene and the last. Unlike the first one, this body was stark naked. Aside from the reddish-gray hair on his head and genitals, the man was fish-belly white. I recognized him as soon as I coned the beam of the flashlight on his face.

"Do you know him?" yelled Captain Morgo.

I nodded.

"He was Dennis Wheatley's best friend. They were roommates here at St. Andrews twenty years ago. His name is Robin Massey."

I saw another difference after leaning farther over the railing to get a better look at his neck.

"He didn't use the concertina wire this time," I called out.

"Who didn't?" yelled Captain Morgo, who was holding on for dear life.

"The man who murdered them," I said after regaining my balance on the walkway. "Maybe he didn't have any more of it."

I wondered what had happened to Robin Massey's clothes. Aside from his white clerical collar, which was wedged into the wire mesh beneath the railing, the only things left were his shoes. It was possible the wind had blown the rest away, or the killer might have thrown them over. Nestled at the base of one of the vertical stanchions, I saw one of the green plastic reunion cups. Picking it up with my gloves, I smelled the same aroma of whiskey that had been in Wheatley's cup.

"The coroner will find that he probably has as much liquor in him as Wheatley did," I shouted over the wind.

"Do you know why?" she shouted back.

"I think they were both forced to drink against their will before he made them walk the railing."

It occurred to me that there was now only one roommate left from the original three, and that was Hoyt Palmer. I had last seen him on his way to the Groton Medical Center in an ambulance. I told Captain Morgo who he was.

"His life could be in danger too," I shouted. "You should contact the Groton police and have a guard put on his room at the medical center. If he's been released, they should take him into protective custody as soon as they locate him."

While she was calling the police dispatcher on her radio, I cradled the flashlight in my armpit and trained it on the acorn-shaped ball at the end of the braided rope. Gazing at it, I felt another twinge of recognition.

Grasping the ball in the fingers of my work glove, I turned it over several times in my hand, examining the braided gold stitching that covered it like tiny cornrows. I suddenly remembered the presentation sword that the army had given me after I had won the Silver Star. The sword now rested next to the hearth of my fireplace, where I used it to poke logs.

The acorn-shaped ball looked like a big sword knot. The use of them came from a time long ago when men actually fought with swords. They would loop a sword knot along with the strap through the handguard so that they wouldn't lose their sword when the blade connected with steel or bone.

But nobody fought with swords anymore. They were used at military weddings and promotion ceremonies. The last time Americans had fought with swords was during the Civil War, and I doubted if our murderer was 175 years old. The concertina wire suggested a military background too. But Wheatley and Massey didn't have any connection to the military.

"What do you think?" yelled Captain Morgo as I continued to study the acorn-shaped ball.

"Do you know what happened to the braided rope that was used in the Wheatley killing?"

"The sheriff's people have it."

I knew that the chances of getting it back anytime soon were slim.

"I know this doesn't follow strict crime scene procedure, but I'd like to cut off this knot and take it with me," I shouted. "There's someone I know who might recognize it."

The old Captain Morgo would have rejected the idea immediately.

"Do it," she came right back.

Using my pocket knife, I sawed through the braided cord and put the ball in my pocket. Standing up, I saw another dark figure coming across the bridge toward us from the direction of the overlook parking lot. I wondered why Ken Macready had let the person past until I saw it was Big Jim Dickey. Indifferent to the swaying bridge, he came strutting up to us like Moses parting the Red Sea.

"This baby is going to be one shit kicker for the record books. I already got three dead over in Enfield," he shouted to us as if thrilled at the growing body count.

Looking down, he saw the clerical collar wedged into the wire mesh. With a steady stream of rain pouring off the brim of his Smokey the Bear hat, he said, "I hear we maybe got us another suicide over here."

Removing her hands from the railing, Captain Morgo turned to face him.

"He was murdered, Sheriff . . . just like the last one," she shouted back almost defiantly. "And I need your criminal investigation team here right away."

Turning to me, she said, "Are you going to the medical center now to interview Mr. Palmer?"

I nodded.

"Take Ken's radio with you. Call me if you need anything."

"Thanks," I said as Big Jim stared at us in obvious confusion.

"And be careful," she admonished me as if I were her prodigal son and had just gotten my first driver's license.

14

I didn't have time to ponder the reasons for Captain Morgo's personality transformation. There was no reason to believe the change would be permanent. For the moment, I was just grateful that something had happened to alter her view of me. At the bridge entrance, I told Ken Macready about Captain Morgo's request, and he turned over his VHF radio.

"There are distress calls coming in from all over the place," he said. "Electricity is out in a lot of the county, and the governor will be declaring us an official disaster area."

I turned off the radio as soon as I was out of sight up the footpath. If I needed it at some point, I wanted to make sure the batteries were still charged and working. As I reached the overlook parking lot, another vehicle pulled in and parked. It was Jordan Langford's Volvo. Walking through the curtain of rain toward it, I wondered who was driving.

The power window on the driver's side slid halfway down as I came up. It was Jordan. In the glow of the interior lights, he looked drawn. There were new pouches under his eyes, and his jaw sagged.

"We've got another one out there on the bridge, I gather," he said almost apprehensively as the slanting rain peppered his windbreaker through the window.

"Yeah. It's Robin Massey, Dennis Wheatley's friend."

Staring straight ahead, he was silent for several seconds.

"I knew Robin," he said with deep sadness in his voice. "The man was a living saint. No one could have wanted to murder him."

"Yeah, well . . . someone did," I said.

He looked up at me for the first time. His eyes tightened as they took in my swollen face. I waited for him to say something but he didn't. I wondered if Blair had told him about my fight.

"Any new leads on Dennis's death?" he asked.

"It's possible the murderer has some kind of military connection. That's one of the things I'm trying to pin down. We also have a video recording of the people at last night's crime scene. I'm going to take a look at it after I've interviewed a guy named Hoyt Palmer. He and Robin Massey were Wheatley's roommates in their last year here."

"What was his name?" he asked.

"Hoyt Palmer."

"I don't remember ever meeting him with Dennis."

"He's lived in Finland for the last twenty years. This afternoon, he was taken to the Groton Medical Center for possible food poisoning."

"I don't have to tell you this . . . but please try to move as fast as you can," he said. "This thing could wreck the college for years to come. I can just see the tabloid coverage now . . . come home to St. Andrews and die."

He still hadn't asked about his own tabloid story.

"How is Blair taking it all?" I asked him.

"She's okay," he said. "Why?"

"Just wondering . . . I assume she knows you well enough to figure out when something's wrong."

"She's fine," he said emphatically.

Apparently, she hadn't confided her visit to me.

My flashlight beam happened to be pointing down at the side of his car when I noticed a raw scar in the paintwork. It ran horizontally across the door and all the way to the rear fender.

"Looks like somebody keyed your car," I said.

He nodded and said, "Who knows why? Blair saw it and pointed it out to me. I have no idea when it happened. Probably some kids."

I remembered the two other cars I had seen with similar gouges when I arrived at the overlook parking lot and found Dennis Wheatley's body.

"Any luck with my own little problem?" he asked forlornly.

His wounded eyes were obviously anticipating bad news.

"Yeah . . . I've made a little progress there."

"You're kidding," he came back, his voice animated for the first time.

"No. I found the men who recorded you at the Wonderland. I've collected all their electronic equipment and possibly some other recorded material. I'll take a quick look at those when I have a chance."

"Thank you, Jake," he said, looking up at me again with his luminous eyes. "Truly."

"Don't thank me yet. I haven't done anything."

"What happened to your face?" he asked.

"The price of progress," I said. "But I don't know yet who hired them to tape you or why. There's still a long way to go."

"You said men. There was more than one?"

"Yeah."

"If it's a matter of priorities, these deaths are far more important."

"They could be connected."

He nodded.

"Do you know a man named Bobby Devane?"

"Never heard of him."

"Do you know anyone at the Razzano law firm?"

"The whiplash brothers?"

I nodded again.

"The older one . . . Brian. He graduated from St. Andrews about twenty years ago . . . I think Dennis Wheatley's class. Since then, he and his brother have made a fortune in divorce work, asbestos, and workers' comp cases. He lives farther down the lake from you at Glenwood Landing . . . one of those huge trophy houses."

"How well do you know him?"

"He's a new member of my board of trustees and has given the school a million dollars. His wife, Dawn, is a good friend of Blair's. We're dedicating the nanoscience learning center in his name next week. Why?"

"Because he or his brother may have paid the men who were hired to film you at the Wonderland. The other possibility is this Bobby Devane. He runs a private detective agency in Syracuse."

I heard a crack like an artillery shell, and the massive oak tree at the end of the parking lot went over with a crunching roar, blocking the road toward campus. Jordan watched it go with almost detached curiosity.

"Do you have a direct number for Razzano?" I asked.

He pulled a cell phone out of his windbreaker pocket. Using a stylus, he punched the screen several times.

"Home okay?" he asked.

I nodded, and he wrote the number down on a notepad he pulled from the glove compartment. Shutting the window, he turned off the engine and got out of the car. While he walked down to the bridge, I headed over to my pickup.

Hearing the thin wail of sirens approaching, I watched as a white panel truck carrying the sheriff's investigative unit arrived. Three men jumped out and began unloading equipment from the rear doors as I headed down the hill.

15

When I reached the bottom of Campus Hill, I saw that two cars had recently collided at the intersection. They still blocked the roadway. In the glare of their dueling headlights, a hulking woman wearing bib overalls and a Tibetan-style goatherder's cap was poking her finger at the second driver, who was dressed like a Gloucester fisherman, with a yellow rain hat and matching slicker.

My wiper blades were fighting a losing battle to clear the windshield as I headed across Groton toward the hospital. A handful of drivers were still braving the elements, crawling along at about the same speed as the people walking bent over on the sidewalks.

At the end of the town square, I crossed over to Seneca Street. A few blocks farther on, the lights of the Groton Medical Center slowly emerged out of the rain. I headed up its treelined macadam driveway.

Built in the early part of the twentieth century, the place always reminded me of the military stockade at Fort Leavenworth, with dirty brick walls and forbidding windows. Up at the college, they were constructing one new building after another, thanks to wealthy alumni like Brian Razzano. But no one was ready to pony up the money for a new hospital.

The driveway that led to the emergency room was choked with vehicles, their yellow lights flashing and their sirens wailing thinly into the savage wind. Driving my pickup right over the curb, I parked it on the grass and headed inside.

A couple dozen people with storm-related injuries already packed the waiting area. A few were lying on rolling gurneys. Others filled the halls flanking the treatment rooms. The newest arrivals were sitting on the floor in the entrance foyer with their backs against the walls.

Several nurses were performing triage evaluations as they worked their way through the crush, sending the most serious cases into the emergency-care stations. When I showed my security badge at the front desk, the woman checked her intake log and told me that Hoyt Palmer had been moved to room 1326.

I trudged up the iron staircase that led to the central wing of the hospital building. On the third floor, a plastic-covered map showed the four nursing stations that could be found at each corner of the rectangular corridor. Room 1326 was on the hallway parallel to the one where I was standing.

Aside from the muted din of the wind and rain, things seemed relatively peaceful on the top floor. At the nursing station closest to room 1326, a Groton police officer was talking to one of the nurses. Behind them, a harried-looking staff doctor was filling out paperwork at a small desk. The individual patient rooms stretched back along a well-lit corridor.

The police officer seemed to shrink in height as I came toward him. Not more than five six, he had the steroid-enhanced development of someone who was out to maximize what little he had.

His neck was almost as large as his head, and his pale-blue uniform was sculpted to fit tightly over every muscle in his arms and legs. A black plastic nameplate above his right breast pocket read, "Schmidt." A Sig Sauer .40 automatic bulged on his narrow hips.

Showing him my campus security badge, I said, "There's a patient in 1326 who is supposed to be under your protective custody. His name is Hoyt Palmer."

"You got any idea how long I'm supposed to be stuck on babysitting duty?" he said, rocking back and forth from heel to toe. "We got a hurricane going on out there, in case you guys up at the college didn't notice."

"Yeah," I said. "It's tough all over. Is your backup in the room with him?"

"Don't need no backup . . . I got it under control."

"Sure," I said, already worried. "How long have you been here?"

"About fifteen minutes. The guy's wife and another lady were in the room with him when I got here. I told him he was being put under police protection just like the sergeant told me to say."

"That must have been comforting to him. Then what?"

"Then he asked me why he needed police protection, and so I told him about the other guy getting waxed in the same place the first guy did," he said.

"So why are you standing out here?" I said.

"'Cause they asked me to leave."

"Yeah," I said. "I can understand that."

He was oblivious to my sarcasm.

"There's no back stairs down at the end of that corridor. The only way anyone can get to him is to come through me."

He bulked out his chest.

"Has anyone come or gone since you got here?" I asked.

"The ladies that were with him left about five minutes ago. Otherwise nobody went down there."

"Have you checked on him since?"

When he shook his head no, I said, "I see you're a regular Dick Tracy."

"What's that supposed to mean?" he demanded.

"It means you're an idiot," I said, heading down the hallway to Palmer's room.

I heard the tap of his heels coming after me.

"I don't have to take your crap," he called out.

Room 1326 was the fifth one down the hallway on the left. The door was closed. I shoved it open and stepped inside the room. The only light came from the wall fixture in the small bathroom, but it was enough to see that the big hospital bed was empty, its top sheet lying on the floor.

Turning on the overhead light, I looked toward the closet. Its plastic accordion door was squeezed open. A white shirt and khaki pants hung from the metal hanger rod. A pair of brown loafers rested on the floor.

"What the hell?" Schmidt said from the doorway.

"So no one came in or out since you've been here," I said, going over to the narrow casement window. "He must have been the invisible man."

The window was closed and latched from the inside.

"So what do you think, Dick?" I demanded.

"I . . . it's impossible," he said.

"Yeah," I said, heading for the door. "If I were you, I'd check every room on this corridor right now. Maybe you'll still have a job in the morning."

When I turned to look back at the end of the hallway, he was pushing open the first door, his Sig Sauer pointed and ready. By then I knew that if someone had been hiding in one of the other rooms, they were already gone.

On the way back to my truck, I thought about the possibilities. What if Hoyt Palmer was the killer? What if he had done it to silence whatever Wheatley and Massey had done to put his life in jeopardy?

16

Checking my watch, I saw it was past five thirty and approaching dawn. Outside, the sky was still dark, but the rain had turned to a fine drizzle, and the wind was definitely slackening a bit. Getting into the truck, I remembered Ken Macready telling me that the hurricane would reach its peak later in the morning. This had to be the eye of the storm passing over us.

The roads around the town square were flooded with six inches of water, and I wondered if the lake might have begun to overflow its banks. Glancing into the rearview mirror, I saw that my pickup was leaving a wake behind me, as if I were trolling for game fish in a power boat.

I imagined Bug waiting for me in our cabin and decided to check on her as soon as I had a chance. What I needed most at that moment was coffee. I hadn't slept more than six hours over the previous three nights and didn't anticipate any change in that situation.

Driving back up Campus Hill, I tried to focus on Hoyt Palmer's disappearance. Even in my worn-out state, I knew that only two things could have happened to him. Either he had left his hospital room voluntarily or the murderer of Wheatley and Massey had taken him out.

I remembered Schmidt saying that nobody had gone down there, which meant that he had probably kept a pretty good watch for anyone trying to get by him in the corridor. But he wouldn't have expected Palmer to slip past him from the other direction.

If it had been abduction and the killer was crafty, he could easily have created a diversion to mask his infiltration of that corridor. I would have. Once in the room, all he had to do was disable Palmer and then wait in one of the other rooms for his chance to leave.

If Palmer had been abducted, it was a likely possibility that he would soon be headed for a rendezvous at the suspension footbridge. The first two deaths were obviously connected, and Palmer was the missing link.

Turning on the VHF transceiver, I reached Captain Morgo and told her that our man had gone missing from his hospital room. I recommended that she issue a missing persons alert for him right away.

She was still at the bridge with the sheriff's investigative unit but agreed to forward the request immediately. Before signing off, I suggested she post guards at both ends of the bridge, and she promised to do so before leaving the murder scene.

Heading across the campus, I passed by the ivy-covered dormitory in which I had lived as a freshman. The college still hadn't lost electrical power, and through the lower windows I could see a boisterous hurricane party taking place. In one of the upper-floor windows, a young coed's face was pressed against the glass as she gazed out at the storm. I waved to her as I went by, but she couldn't have seen me.

A big sycamore tree had fallen against a side wall of the campus police building, and a team of men with chainsaws were cutting it away. Pulling into the rear parking lot, I parked in Captain Morgo's spot by the back door.

After unlocking the tool chest secured behind the cab of my truck, I pulled out the surveillance equipment that I had found in Sal's room at the Wonderland Motel and took it inside.

Every desk in the squad room was occupied by security officers or members of the college's emergency deployment team, all of them fielding phone calls or dispatching assistance. A handful of folding cots had been set up along the walls, and several officers in rain-soaked uniforms were sacked out on them.

I needed somewhere private to view the videos and decided to use Lieutenant Ritterspaugh's empty office on the second floor. The room was dark and tinged with the aroma of her incense burner. Setting the surveillance equipment on her desk, I went back down to the squad room and poured myself a big mug of black coffee, chugging it as I stood there.

My mind was tracking about as well as the woolly mammoth over in Duffield Hall. There was only so much that coffee could do for me after all the adrenaline I had expended in the last twenty-four hours.

In Afghanistan, I had often used amphetamines to get through nightlong stakeouts, but I wasn't about to ask for one now. I glanced across the squad room. The cots along the far wall began to look like the presidential suite at the Hay-Adams. I poured myself another mug of coffee.

On my way back upstairs, I passed Ken Macready in the hallway and asked him to bring the camcorder material he had shot at the Wheatley crime scene up to the lieutenant's office.

As I was connecting the recording equipment to a television monitor, another rending crack was followed by a deafening thud that made the floor tremble. Another sycamore, its shallow roots loosened in the mushy soil, had gone over.

A few moments later, Ken brought the disc into the office and handed it to me. As he was heading out the door, an idea suddenly registered in my head, and I put down the connector cables.

"Ken . . . when I got here yesterday morning, there were two kids sitting downstairs in the holding pen," I said. "Check the arrest log and find out what they were initially charged with before their lawyer got here."

"Yes, sir."

"I think it's about time you started calling me Jake."

He was grinning as he went out the door.

Fortunately, the camcorder video was digital. One of the electronic components in Sal's metal case was a mini digital video player. I finished connecting it to the back of the television monitor and put in the disc.

The action lasted only about three minutes, and the little bald man had shot some of the first vivid footage. He could have gotten a pile of money for it from one of the TV tabloid news shows. *Billionaire Decapitated—Fun for the Whole Family.* There was a dramatic close-up of Wheatley's body as it was falling, followed by my frantic efforts to grab his head before it followed the rest of him down the gorge.

The next images were of me as I sprinted toward the command car. The footage stopped abruptly at the point when I grabbed the camera out of his hands. The last two minutes consisted of Ken panning the camera around the small crowd of observers who were standing at the overlook.

I had finished running it the first time when he stepped back into the office.

"Those two boys you asked about," he said. "They were charged with vandalism, malicious mischief, and destruction of private property."

"Did the log indicate what they had actually done?"

He nodded. "They were caught defacing some cars with screwdrivers over at the administration building. Their lawyer is apparently a local hotshot. He's trying to get the charges dropped by promising full financial restitution to the victims."

"What time were they arrested?" I asked.

"According to the log, it was three thirty in the morning."

"How old are they?"

"Eleven and twelve."

I would have gone directly to their homes and interviewed them separately, but there was no time. After telling Ken about the keyed cars I had seen in the overlook parking lot on the night of Wheatley's death, I said, "Call their parents and explain that those kids could be material witnesses in the investigation. Tell them that if they bring them here right away, I'll do my best to help get their charges reduced. When they get here, separate them."

"Done," he said.

I rewound Ken's section of the footage and played it again. Unfortunately, most of the people who had gathered at the overlook to rubberneck the tragedy were standing in the shadows far away from the streetlamps. In the pale reflection of the blue emergency light, I was able to recognize the little bald man who owned the camera, as well as the two pot-bellied alumni who had recognized me. Of the remaining dozen or so figures, about half were women. The other faces went by in a murky blur.

At one point, Ken had swung the camera in a wider arc and caught the cars parked at the lower edge of the parking lot. The camera didn't linger at any point, and all the images sped by. When I played it a third time, however, my eyes were drawn to a figure illuminated against the backdrop of the evergreen trees that fringed the lot.

The fourth time through, I hit the pause button as soon as the panning motion began. By continually punching the pause button, I was able to see each image as it unfolded, a split second apart.

As the footage arrived at the evergreen trees, there was a momentary flare of light as a car or police vehicle went by on the street. For just that moment, it illuminated the trees. I kept the last frozen image on the television monitor for almost ten seconds.

Not only was it possible to see the human face peering through the branches of the trees, but there was no doubt who it was. I had spent too many hours with him over the years not to recognize his craggy features.

It was Ben Massengale, the fallen hero who had inspired me to make the army my career way back when I was in the ROTC program at St. Andrews. He could have been rubbernecking like the rest of the onlookers. Word would have spread fast down to the Creeker. At the same time, he was still wiry and strong. And he was an expert with military accouterments.

17

The office windows began rattling like castanets, and I knew the storm was rising in intensity again. I ejected Ken's camcorder disc from the video player and pulled out the two unlabeled recordings I had found in Sal's metal carrying case. I inserted the first one in the player and pushed the start button.

Like the one of Jordan and the girl, it was an amateur production. This one featured an old white-haired gentleman and a pimply teenage boy. They were both naked. The boy was almost cadaverously skinny. The old man had a grotesque stomach paunch that looked like a bloated tumor.

It had been shot at night, and the action took place in a blue Jacuzzi tub that was set flush into a wooden deck. In the background, I could see an open sliding glass door that led into the family room of a contemporary home.

The two participants in the foreground didn't waste any time demonstrating their sexual orientation, and it didn't appear that either was aware they were being filmed. About five minutes into the action, I stopped the recording and ejected it.

The second revealed another sexual encounter. This one was filmed in daylight. It looked as though it might have been shot somewhere in the Adirondacks. Through the bedroom window in the video, I could see snowcapped peaks. There were three participants, two of them women.

The man on the bed looked familiar to me. He appeared to be in his late sixties and in good physical condition. He needed to be. The two young blondes in bed with him were each giving him enough action for a newlywed.

I ejected the disc and placed all three of them in Sal's metal case, which I shoved under Lieutenant Ritterspaugh's desk. There were probably other scintillating episodes on Sal's videos, but I didn't have time to review them.

Sal had told me the truth when he said he wasn't working for the Wonderland Motel, but he hadn't been recording just Jordan Langford. The net was obviously wider and almost certainly involved other blackmail efforts.

Ken Macready appeared in the doorway.

"Jake, one of the boys you asked me to find is waiting outside in the corridor," he said. "His father is a housemaster in one of the freshman dorms. He brought him right over."

"What about the second boy?" I asked.

"When I spoke to his father, he said his son wasn't guilty of anything and that he was being harassed because of his political views."

"The political views of a boy?"

"I guess the father's," said Ken. "He's the Tea Party guy who made the public statements about the Jews and Communists taking over Groton."

I knew which one was his son.

"Bring the other boy in," I said. "Tell his father to wait outside."

As I expected, it was the Pillsbury Doughboy with curly red hair and pasty skin. He wasn't crying this time, but his hands were trembling as he came into the office. I told him to sit down in the chair by the desk.

The boy was dressed in what he had been wearing in the holding pen: NBA jersey, gold chain, baggy jeans, and basketball sneakers. His cap was still jauntily cocked to the right side.

"What's your name, son?" I asked gently.

"Cody . . . McNamara," he said uncertainly.

"Cody, I'm told that you were arrested for vandalizing several cars in the parking lot of the campus administration building. Did you do that?"

I needed to find out right away how truthful he was going to be.

"Yeah . . . we did it," he confessed. "Brett and me."

"Thanks for being honest with me, Cody. Now this next question is really important. Last night, did you boys gouge some cars in the overlook parking lot, the one next to the suspension footbridge?"

His eyes immediately dropped to his lap. Almost ten seconds passed before he began to slowly move his head up and down.

"All right, then," I said. "Cody, I guess you know by now that someone died there that night."

He nodded again but refused to look at me.

"Will you tell me what you saw at the bridge?"

A small flood of tears began to flow out of his eyes and roll down his apple cheeks. They came together at the point of his chin and dropped down onto the links of the gold-plated chain around his neck. I was about to pose the question again but decided to wait.

As the seconds passed, it suddenly came to me who the second man had been in Sal's sex videos, the one with the two cheap blondes. The last time I had seen him, he was the presiding judge in a state supreme court chamber.

I had been in court representing the St. Andrews campus police department. We were one of the defendants in a liability lawsuit brought by a student who claimed she had gotten ill from asbestos poisoning after living in one of the older dorms.

The man cavorting like a sex-starved porpoise was Supreme Court Justice Addison Davis. I was still trying to remember the name of the law firm that had filed the suit on behalf of the girl when Cody McNamara spoke again.

"Me and Brett were coming back toward campus after hanging out by one of the sorority houses on the other side of the gorge," he said in a wavering voice. "Both of us had our screwdrivers in our pockets and, uh . . . uh . . . we decided to key the first couple of cars in the lot."

He stopped to wipe his nose with the back of his hand before going on.

"We were still there by the cars, and it was real dark. I told Brett I didn't want to stay out any longer, and he started calling me a pussy and a faggot. That's when I saw something moving down by that phone box that has the blue light over it. I grabbed Brett's arm, and he looked down there too. This one guy was helping another guy down the path to the bridge," he continued. "The other guy looked really sick. I mean, he couldn't walk so good on his own, and the first guy had to practically hold him up as they went down there. When they got under the blue light, I saw that the first guy had something over his shoulder . . . a rolled-up garden hose like . . . and then they went out onto the bridge."

"What did you see after that?" I asked.

"That was it. That was all I saw."

"What did you do then?"

"Brett said we ought to go down there and find out what they were doing . . . but I . . . I just wanted to go home. So when he started walking down toward the footbridge, I began walking the long way around. He must have decided to follow me because he caught up in a few seconds and we both went that way."

It made sense. The boy lived in the housemaster's apartment in one of the freshman dorms, which were on the opposite side of the campus. The administration building where they had keyed the other cars was on the way.

"Can you describe the first man, Cody . . . the one with the garden hose around his shoulders?"

"It was really dark," said the boy, "but he was big compared to the other guy."

"How big?"

Looking up at me, he said, "Like you . . . maybe even taller."

Ben Massengale was taller than me.

Standing up, I went out into the hallway and thanked Mr. McNamara for coming into the office. I pledged to see what I could do to help Cody when his case came up in juvenile court. As soon as they were gone, I sat down again and rested my head on the cushioned ergonomic pad on Lieutenant Ritterspaugh's desk.

I knew I had to find Ben Massengale, but first I spent a few minutes thinking about what I could still do to resolve Jordan's other predicament. If I couldn't find and then confront the blackmailer, he would be resigning in less than twelve hours. Whoever was demanding the five million dollars had to know about the Wheatley gift sitting in Jordan's private discretionary account. *Why only five?* I wondered. Why not ten or twenty?

Had the blackmailer arranged to kill Wheatley because Wheatley was the only one in a position to know that Jordan had the money and could do whatever he wanted with it?

Who would have had access to the information aside from Jordan?

The questions kept turning over in my mind like an ancient cement mixer. Raising my bleary head from the elbow pad, I looked up at the wall clock. It was twenty after six, and the wind was climbing again on the decibel scale. The sky through the window was a weird metallic color.

I came up with two ideas. They probably weren't going to do any good, but I decided to act on them anyway. Digging into the breast pocket of my waterproof jacket, I found the business card for Bobby Devane. Picking up the phone, I called the cell number that was scrawled on the back of it. The number rang five times before kicking over to his voice mailbox.

"This is Robert Devane," came a low raspy voice. "Leave a message."

So I left him a message.

"This is Jake Cantrell in Groton, Bobby. I was the one who met Sal and Angie at the Wonderland. I'm enjoying all that illegal surveillance equipment of yours . . . especially the blackmail videos. Sal was kind enough to tell me what you hired him to do. So before I have you arrested for extortion, Bobby, I thought we should probably talk. Give me a call."

I left him my extension number at the campus police department and hung up. Unlike the cabin phone, it had a feature that kicked straight back to the dispatcher if I wasn't there.

Next, I dug out the home number Jordan had given me for Brian Razzano. It rang only twice before someone picked it up.

"Razzano," said a baritone voice. I recognized it from all the TV commercials.

"My name is Jake Cantrell," I began. "I live down the lake from you and work in the campus security office at St Andrews College."

"Jake Cantrell," he slowly repeated, as if pondering a name from the distant past. I was struck by the fact that he didn't seem remotely surprised by my calling him at six thirty in the morning in the middle of a hurricane.

"Not the immortal Tank Cantrell?"

"Yeah . . . good old Tank," I said.

"I was in the stands when you broke through the line against Tulane and ran for the winning touchdown," he reminisced. "You were dragging two guys on your back there at the end and—"

Interrupting him, I said, "Your name was given to me as someone who employs a man named Bobby Devane in confidential investigations. Last night, I met two of his employees at the Wonderland Motel up near the thruway. They had electronic surveillance equipment in their room, and they have been filming people in intimate situations who apparently had no knowledge of it. Personally I think you're heading the blackmail operation, Mr. Razzano, and if I give what I already know to the *New York Times*, they'll be scraping your name off the front of the campus nanoscience center before the chisel is even dry."

I was wincing over the mixed metaphor when he shouted, "For God's sake, what are you talking about?"

"I'm sure you already know, Brian," I said. "How about the Honorable Justice Addison Davis for one? You ever see the good judge naked and being sandwiched between two blondes?"

I hung up the phone as a branch hurtled against the upper panes of the office window. It remained suspended there for a few seconds before being swept away by the wind.

Only time would tell if my poking a stick into the two beehives would produce any live stingers. In the meantime, I had to find Ben Massengale. I had a pretty good idea where he would be.

18

On my way out to the parking lot, I had to climb over the trunk of one of the downed sycamores. Its gnarled muddy roots filled the air with a raw earthy smell, as if Mother Nature was starting to sweat from her vast labors in turning the world upside down.

I turned on the news in the truck and learned that Hurricane Ilse had been downgraded to Category Two. It seemed like she had forgotten to tell us in Groton. I heard another crescendo of thunder, and the sky went darker as rain came down like a curtain.

The main road across the campus was empty except for a careening garbage can and whirling clouds of autumn leaves. Near the traffic bridge, I saw a newly downed power line. Yellow sparks were shooting out of its exposed end as the wire whipped back and forth across the road like a demented rattlesnake. Turning on the radio transceiver, I reported it to the campus security dispatcher.

When I pulled into the parking lot at the Fall Creek Tavern, I was surprised to see it still had power. It stood out against the craggy gorge like the beacon of a lighthouse.

Near the precipice, the wind was gusting at sixty or seventy miles an hour.

Bent over, I was heading toward the side entrance when I heard several loud cracks followed by what sounded like muffled hammer blows. The noises were coming from the Creeker's foundation wall. I knelt in the lee of the wind to take a closer look.

I was no mechanical engineer, but it looked like the bottom support timbers of the building had just shifted on the stone foundation. Along the mortared foundation wall, I could see four inches of newly exposed surface, still untouched by the driving rain. A few moments later, it was soaked as dark as the rest.

When I stepped inside the bar, the blast of the wind was muted by the amplified noise of blaring rap music. At least a hundred people crowded the big downstairs room, packed together from the open kitchen to the back pool table area that extended out over the edge of the gorge.

I found the owner, Chuck McKinlay, sitting at a table near the smoky fireplace. Over the jukebox, I had to lean down to tell him what I had just seen outside. He gazed tranquilly back up at me, his eyes vacant with single malt.

"The Creeker's been here since before my grandfather was born," he shouted, as if that answered my question.

"You should check it out, Chuck," I urged before heading off to look for Ben Massengale.

Before I took two steps, Johnny Joe Splendorio emerged out of the crush in front of me.

"Jake," he yelled over the noise, his cheeks flushed burgundy red. "I got something good for you."

I scanned the crowd at the bar, hoping to find Ben on his favorite stool.

"The Gambian pouched rat," he said close to my ear. "They grow to fifteen pounds . . . big as raccoons, and they eat anything . . . I mean birds, cats, garbage scraps . . . best of all, you can fight 'em like pit bulls. The goddamn Latinos will love them."

Ben wasn't sitting or standing at the bar, and I began pushing through the crowd toward the room in the back. Johnny Joe stuck close behind me.

"I'm raising the money for the first shipment, Jake," he yelled. "Buy a hundred and they're only twenty a piece. I figure we can sell 'em for fifty each."

"Where have you been?" a sharp voice came from over my shoulder.

It was Kelly. A tray of empty beer bottles was balanced above her right hand.

"I've been trying to reach you since yesterday," she said.

Seeing the look on her face, Johnny Joe wisely retreated. When Kelly took in the cuts around my eyes and my swollen jaw, her eyes softened.

"Oh, Jake," she said, still balancing the tray in one hand while stroking my face with her left.

"Kelly, I don't have any time to tell you what's going on," I said. "You have to trust me that it's important."

"Those two killings everyone's talking about?" she asked with an involuntary shudder.

I nodded.

"Have you seen Ben Massengale since last night?" I asked her.

"He was here," she said. "He was talking with somebody at the bar for the longest time. The guy may have run him home."

"What did the man look like?"

She pursed her lips for a few moments and said, "God . . . with everything going on Jake, I can't remember."

"If he comes in again, please call the campus police dispatcher and have them contact me on my radio. I'm heading down to his apartment."

"Jake," she called out, and I swung around.

"Be careful, honey," she said with an apprehensive smile.

I remembered the problem I had seen outside and said, "Kelly, I think this building is starting to move on its foundation. Chuck is too drunk to care, but it could be dangerous. Use my name and call the Groton emergency line. Tell them to send one of their building engineers over here right away. Be sure to tell them it's an emergency."

"Don't worry, Jake. I'll take care of it," she said, raising her lips for a quick good-bye kiss.

Outside, the force of the wind was steadier and more violent. Driving down Campus Hill, my headlights almost disappeared in the torrential rain as it swept the windshield.

More than a foot of standing water now flooded the downtown streets. Abandoned cars sat stranded at nearly every intersection. I drove past the town square and traveled the three blocks along Seneca Street to where Ben lived.

It was a neighborhood of rundown Victorian houses that had been turned into illegal apartments for transient workers. Electrical power had been knocked out on the street, and Ben's house was dark when I pulled up at the curb. Unhooking my flashlight, I waded across his inundated lawn and climbed the sagging wooden stairs that led up to the porch.

A faded card on one of the mailboxes attached to the wall read, "B. Massengale: Apt. 3C."

The front door of the building stood wide open. The wind-driven rain had already soaked the foyer of the hallway. Closing the door behind me, I smelled the sour odor of wet plaster.

A section of the ceiling above the foyer was leaking badly in several places, and water was splattering down in a steady rhythm on the hardwood flooring. Training the flashlight ahead of me, I headed up the staircase to his room.

As the rickety stairs creaked and groaned, I felt a small tremor of apprehension. To minimize the noise I was making, I placed my boots at the butt end of each step. On the third floor, I made my way down the dark hallway and approached Ben's door. I thought about knocking but decided against it. Although it was hard to believe he was the killer, it remained a possibility. And he might not be alone.

The door was made of pressed fiberboard. Keeping the flashlight in my left hand, I removed the .45 automatic from its holster with my right. I waited another five seconds and kicked the door open, shattering the lock at the doorjamb.

The first room of the apartment was his kitchen. An assortment of pizza boxes and empty liquor bottles covered the drainboard next to the sink. Crossing the floor, I went down a narrow hallway. An open door on the left led into a living room that overlooked the street. There was a sprung leather chair by the window next to a small coffee table crowded with more empty liquor bottles.

The last door on the right was closed. Turning the knob, I slowly pushed it open. The window curtains were drawn shut, and the room was pitch black. I inched my eyes around the edge of the doorjamb and shined my flashlight inside.

Dirty clothes lay strewn across the floor. I found the bed in the beam of the flashlight. Ben was lying on his side, his face to the wall. I slowly walked over to him. He didn't move.

Standing over him, I saw the regular swelling of his chest and stomach as he breathed in and out. The odor in the room was awful, like a bear's den after a long winter. A bear addicted to cheap whiskey.

I walked across to his bathroom and shined the light inside. Aside from an old Marine Corps bathrobe hanging on the wall hook, it was empty. A photograph was Scotch-taped to the mirror over the sink. It was a picture of his late wife, Karin, and must have been taken around the time I was a student at St. Andrews. She looked back at me, as lovely as Julia Roberts.

I remembered the barbecues she and Ben had held for the ROTC students on Sunday afternoons in the backyard of their little house near the campus. We all thought he was the luckiest guy on the planet. The house was gone now, just as she was. They had torn it down to build one of the new learning centers.

Putting the .45 back in its holster, I pulled open the heavy curtains that covered the windows. In the murky morning light, I saw another empty whiskey bottle lying under Ben's outstretched arm. The Seagram's label was facing toward me. I wondered if that might have been what Wheatley had been drinking before he went off the bridge.

"Ben," I said loudly, shaking his shoulder.

He erupted in a bout of tubercular coughing before rolling over in the bed to face the other way.

"Ben," I called out to him again.

His eyes slowly opened and took me in.

"S'you, Jake?" he mumbled.

"Yeah."

Going into the bathroom, I found a fruit jar on the sink. Rinsing it out, I filled it with tap water. After helping Ben to sit up, I held the glass to his mouth, and he gulped most of it down. When I took my hand away from his shoulder, he slumped back on the pillow.

In spite of his once prodigious strength, it was hard for me to visualize him on the suspension footbridge, doing what was physically required to hang two men against their will.

"Ben, I need your help," I said, propping him up with his back against the pillowed headboard.

His head lolled forward, but he tried to focus his eyes. I pulled out the golden ball I had cut off the end of the braided rope from my breast pocket and held it up to him.

"Do you know what this is, Ben?"

He had taught the military etiquette class in the ROTC program.

"Sword . . . knot," he said.

"Ever seen one that looks exactly like this before?" I asked next.

He continued to examine it through bleary eyes.

"Genrals," he said, slurring the word.

"Generals?" I repeated.

"Genral's . . . acorn . . . other officers . . . tassels," he said, exhaling the sour odor of stale whiskey.

"How did you get home last night, Ben?"

He thought about it for ten seconds before finally saying, "Can't remember, Jake."

"Kelly said you were talking to someone for a long time last night. Can you remember who it was?"

His confused eyes were still focused on the acorn knot in my hand.

"Five . . . oh . . . deuce," he muttered.

"You're not making sense, Ben."

"Five . . . oh . . . deuce," he slurred again. "One oh . . . fist."

"The 101st?"

His bloodshot eyes started to close and then briefly fluttered open again.

"You got a drink on ya, Jake?" he asked.

I shook my head no. A few seconds later, his chin dropped to his chest and he began to snore.

19

The flood in the streets of Groton had risen to more than two feet. As I headed back across town, it began sloshing into the cab of my pickup through the spaces around the brake, clutch, and gas pedals.

A silver-and-gold Humvee with vanity plates lay abandoned in the middle of Buffalo Street. They don't make trucks the way they used to. I navigated past it like an ocean tug.

Based on the depth of the floodwaters, I knew that the lake level must have reached the first floor of my cabin. That wouldn't frighten Bug. Nothing would frighten her.

A torrent of muddy water was coursing down the steep grade of Campus Hill, carrying the detritus of the storm along with it. Where it met the standing water at the intersection of Seneca Street, the cataract created a maelstrom more than three feet deep. The water in the cab rose to my ankles as the pickup plowed through it in first gear.

I checked my watch. It was almost eight o'clock. Taking the radio from my belt, I reached Captain Morgo through one of the office dispatchers. She was back at the campus security building, running the emergency rescue operation. Incredibly, her personality transplant appeared to be holding.

"Are you all right?" she demanded.

"I'm fine," I said and asked if the sheriff's investigative team had found anything important at the murder scene. They hadn't reported back to her yet, but she promised to let me know if anything new was discovered.

Hoyt Palmer was still missing. She had sent an officer to check out the Tau Epsilon Rho house in case he might be hiding there from the killer. Palmer's wife was riding out the storm at the fraternity with Evelyn Wheatley. The officer reported that both of them appeared reasonably calm.

"What year did Dennis Wheatley graduate?" I asked.

"Wait a second," she said. The radio went dead for almost a minute.

"1986," she came back.

"I want you to call the *St. Andrews Sun* and tell them I'm coming right over there."

"They don't publish the student paper on Sunday," she said. "There won't be anyone in the office."

I remembered the card that Lauren Kenniston had given me. I fished it out and called the cell number printed under her name. She answered the phone on the second ring.

"Officer Cantrell, I presume," came her voice. "I thought you would be calling me at some point."

"I need your help," I said. "Can you meet me at the *Groton Journal* office?"

"I'm here now," she said. "We have emergency power from our backup generator."

"I'll be there in five minutes."

The *Groton Journal* was located in a stone building on high ground near the foot of Campus Hill. The old Chevy chugged back across town, and I found a place to park on the street in front of the building.

The front door was unlocked. I stepped inside and closed it against the wind. There were lights on over a reception desk.

"'Give me the wretched refuse of your teeming shore,'" said a mellow voice beyond the counter. "'Send these, the tempest-tossed to me.'"

She was standing next to one of the computer terminals in the small news room.

"I might have a lead to identify the man who carried out those hangings," I said.

"Do I get an exclusive?" she asked.

"Sure," I said, "if it leads anyplace."

"Promise?"

"Promise," I said.

"How can I help?"

"I need to look for a story in one of the back issues of the paper."

"Easy. We have every issue cross-indexed in our computer files."

"Going how far back?"

"To 1995, I believe."

"Not far enough," I said. "What about 1986?"

"In the morgue," she said, pointing to the head of an iron staircase. "The hard copies are stored down there."

She led me down the steps and along a dark corridor. Below ground, the sound of the wind was reduced to a moaning growl. When she turned on an overhead fluorescent light, there were two inches of standing water on the basement floor.

Cardboard folders containing past issues of the tabloid-sized newspaper lined long rows of built-in wooden shelving. Despite a large humming dehumidifier, they gave off an odor of mildew and decay.

Bending almost double to avoid the cobwebs, Lauren disappeared behind the second row of shelves, reemerging thirty seconds later with a thick cardboard-bound folder in each hand.

"These cover January 1986," she said, laying the two collections on a big metal table under the fluorescent fixture.

As I opened the first one, she went back to the shelves and returned a minute later with two more.

"Why not tell me what we're looking for."

"I'm not sure, but it will likely be a story involving a traumatic incident at St. Andrews, possibly a death, and may involve one of three students."

I gave her the names of Dennis Wheatley, Robin Massey, and Hoyt Palmer, and she jotted them down on an index card before opening the folder in front of her.

My folder started in the first week of January. After scrolling carefully through each paper, I realized why they called these places morgues. Major news stories I had largely forgotten were uncovered page by page as if fresh and new, interspersed with stories of local or campus interest.

A man named Bernard Goetz was on trial for murder after shooting four young men in a New York subway train. A fire in one of the St. Andrews dormitories forced three students to find new lodging. UCLA beat Iowa 45–28 in the Rose Bowl. The cost of the student dining plan went up 4 percent. Two Sikhs remained on trial in India for murdering President Indira Gandhi. The girls' basketball team lost to Marist. Street riots against "Baby Doc" Duvalier broke out in Port-au-Prince, Haiti. A campus protest drew forty-two students in opposition to President Reagan's Star Wars program.

After fifteen minutes, I still wasn't through the last week of January.

"I think we should just stick to the front pages," I said. "If it was an important story, we should find it there."

She nodded at me and turned a page as another peal of thunder cracked in the world above us. The lights flickered and went off.

"'Trees uptorn, darkness and worms and shrouds and sepulchers,'" came her voice across the table, utterly calm. "John Keats," she added.

"Very comforting," I said.

"At Princeton I majored in English literature."

I switched on the flashlight I was carrying in the side pocket of my waterproof jacket. "Let's take the other sets upstairs."

Up on the first floor, the morning sky was still dark. The backup generator had apparently broken down, and one of the reporters went off to try to find someone who knew how to operate it. We carried the folders over to an oak library table that was positioned under one of the windows.

I checked my watch. It was quarter to nine. After another five minutes of roaming the headlines, my addled brain began to shut down, and I lost my ability to concentrate on the job at hand. I stopped to rub my exhausted eyes. The whole thing looked impossible, and I was about to throw in the towel when Lauren Kenniston said, "I think I might have found something."

She turned the thick folder toward me, and I read the headline and news story.

Student Is Apparent Suicide

The identity of a St. Andrews student whose body was discovered at the bottom of the Fall Creek Gorge yesterday afternoon was officially released today by the Groton Police Department. According to a police spokesman, Jill Watkins, a second-year student majoring in astronomy, left a note taped to the railing of the bridge before taking her life.

Although the contents of the note were
not publicly released, a police spokesman declared that Watkins was despondent over the death of her parents in
December.

"I don't think so," I said wearily. "The circumstances don't
match up."

We went back to the February folders.

OPEC set the price of crude oil at fifteen dollars a barrel.
"Baby Doc" Duvalier had fled from Haiti. A St. Bernard gave
birth to seven puppies in the rock garden behind Duffield Hall.
Ferdinand Marcos and his wife, Imelda, fled the Philippines for
Hawaii. Anatoly Sharansky was freed by President Gorbachev
after eight years in a Soviet labor camp. Students protested a
proposed increase in yearly tuition costs to three thousand
dollars.

"I've found another one," she said from across the table.

She turned the book around and faced me again.

Second Apparent Suicide Rocks Campus

Groton police sergeant Robert Fabbricatore announced today that a St. Andrews
student apparently took his life yesterday morning at the Fall Creek suspension
bridge. The death occurred less than

two weeks after the suicide of sophomore Jill Watkins at the same bridge.

The dead student was identified as
Creighton Taylor, a freshman from Fort
Campbell, Kentucky. An applied econom-
ics major, he was a recent pledge of
the Tau Epsilon Rho fraternity. Sergeant
Fabbricatore did not rule out the possibility that the two deaths were related.

"You might have found it," I said.

Creighton Taylor had been a new member of Wheatley's fraternity. And there was another possible connection. The boy was
from Fort Campbell, Kentucky. The 101st Airborne Division was
based at Fort Campbell. I remembered Ben making the drunken
reference to it before he passed out.

"There doesn't appear to be a follow-up story," said Lauren,
who was still combing the newspapers.

"We already have enough to check further," I said.

Grabbing the transceiver radio from my belt, I called Captain Morgo.

"I've found a possible connection to the murders," I said. "It's
important to find out everything you can in regard to the death
of a student at the suspension footbridge on February twelfth,
1986. His name was Creighton Taylor, and he was from Fort
Campbell, Kentucky. His death was apparently ruled a suicide at

the time. Try to find out if his parents are still living. Call me as soon as you learn anything."

"Will do," she said, signing off.

I had been watching Lauren Kenniston as I related the information. It struck me that she was a very attractive woman as I stood up from the library table.

"Now you know everything I do," I said. "When this is over, I'll buy you dinner."

"You might want to take a rest, Jake," she said to my retreating back. "I don't think you'll get much farther."

"I'm half Irish," I said, turning to grin at her. "If you want to see real exhaustion, just visit me on a typical Sunday morning."

"This is Sunday morning," she said.

20

Back in the truck, I checked my watch. It was 10:35. I figured it would take Captain Morgo at least thirty minutes to track down the information I requested. There was time enough for me to go back to the cabin and check on Bug.

As I drove home, I wondered what had happened to all the St. Andrews alumni who had descended on the campus for homecoming weekend, wanting nothing more than being able to enjoy a football game in the crescent, meet some old friends in familiar haunts, and check out the old girlfriend from freshman year. Now they were probably holed up in their rooms, praying that the hurricane would finally let up so they could go back to their real lives.

Remembering the depth of the floodwater at the bottom of Campus Hill, I decided to drive home the long way around LaFeber Point. It coursed along the hills overlooking the west end of town and brought me back to the lake road about a half mile past the cabin.

Driving along the bluff, the only lights I could see came from the hospital, which like the college and the Groton Police Department, had its own backup generating system in case of a power failure. The rain was still coming hard. Several cars were abandoned along the lake road, the last less than fifty feet from my driveway.

Pulling in, I saw that another white spruce had toppled over. It was leaning precariously against one of the oaks that flanked my cabin, its long green branches almost covering the path to the back door. I parked well away from it.

In the shadowy gloom, I could see that the lake had risen to the level of the front porch. It was too dim too see exactly how far. I pushed aside several large spruce boughs to reach the cabin door.

I remembered having locked it when I left. Switching on the flashlight, I inserted my key, unlocked the dead bolt, and shoved it open. There was an inch of lake water on the cabin floor.

I stopped short. Instinctively, I knew that if Bug was able to walk, she would have been there in front of me. I threw the flashlight inside the open doorway and dove to the left.

As I hit the ground, my right side lit up on fire. The shot had come from the kitchen. Whoever had fired it was using a silencer. If I hadn't thrown the flashlight away from me in the dark, the bullet would probably have taken me in the chest. Bent over, I scrabbled toward the far corner of the cabin.

I wondered if two men had been sent to do the job. No. If there had been more than one, the second killer would have been positioned outside and finished me right away.

I knelt in the wet grass and tried to assess how bad the wound was. I didn't feel faint or dizzy. I could still move. The white heat in my right side was replaced by a steady throbbing ache.

Probing the warm wetness with my fingertips, I realized how lucky I had been. The bullet had passed through the fleshy area above my right hip, managing to miss both the pelvic bone and the lower rib cage before it tore through flesh and muscle and exited out my back.

Cold rain was running down the back of my neck, and it felt soothing somehow. An image of my uncle Bob hurtled into my brain. He was sitting near the fire in our hunting camp with a pint of Wild Turkey in his lap. Rain was hammering the roof of our tent.

"Never try to go hunting in the rain, son," he had said. "You can't hear a goddamn thing."

I pulled out the .45 and cocked it. Staying close to the cabin wall, I crept around the back corner. Lake water was lapping against the stone foundation a few feet away. Floating at its edge was a foot-long square of cedar shake that the wind had ripped away from someone's cottage. After retrieving it, I crawled back to the first of the two living room windows. I slowly raised my eyes to peer over the sill. It was dark inside the room.

Fitting the edge of the shingle into the base of the window frame, I shoved hard from below, and the windowpane groaned upward several inches. A moment later, two holes starred the glass, quickly followed by a third.

From the size of the holes, I knew it had to be a small-caliber gun, maybe a .25, no larger than a .32. I scrabbled quickly along the cabin wall to the smaller living room window next to the fireplace. The lake water was over my boots as I knelt below it and shoved upward again with the shingle.

With a sharp tinkle, two more holes appeared in one of the glass panes. I waited a couple seconds, thrust the muzzle of the Colt over the sill, and squeezed off two rounds into the room.

I didn't expect to hit him, and I wasn't trying to make him expend his ammunition. Unless he was an idiot, I had to assume he would have spare magazines, just as I did. But unlike me, he wasn't bleeding, and I needed to stop him quickly.

I wanted him unsure of where I would come from next. Reversing direction, I staggered back to the first window I had forced open, extended the muzzle through the opening, and fired two more rounds.

It was now or never. I took off around the corner with long strides, lurching for the still open back door. Reaching it, I launched myself headfirst into the kitchen, coming up hard against the side of the refrigerator. Dropping to my belly, I pointed the .45 at the dark passageway to the living room.

The dark blur of him came tearing through the passageway a moment later. He was firing as he came, the bullets going *Phut . . . phut . . . phut*. One of them ricocheted off an iron skillet hanging on a peg over my head. I fired three times into the dark blur. It skidded across the kitchen floor, stopping when it hit the edge of the stove.

I kept a spare flashlight on one of the kitchen shelves. Standing up, I shined it across the room. The man's arms were flung forward over his head. Although his back was to me, I knew who it was as soon as I saw the splint that had been used to bind his dislocated elbow.

A small automatic was still clutched in his right hand. I crawled over and took it away from him. It was a .25 Beretta with a three-inch silencer screwed into the barrel. The original James Bond gun. No stopping power, but good enough for an execution.

Sal Scalise was dead when I turned him over on his back. The water covering the kitchen floor around him slowly turned a tawny red. Two of my .45s had torn holes through his chest, and another had caught him in the stomach. In the beam of the flashlight, his open eyes stared up at the white plaster ceiling as if it held the secrets of the universe.

Looking down at his body, I saw that Bug had done her best for me. There was a long jagged tear in his left pant leg, probably from the greeting she had given him when he broke into the cabin. There were also deep bite marks in his right hand, and her fangs had torn off a long strip of flesh along his thumb.

It was his shooting hand, and he had been forced to wrap it in a bloody handkerchief that was still tied around his palm. It had to have affected his aim. Bug had probably saved my life again.

I stood up and went looking for her. She was out on the porch, lying on her side with the cold lake water lapping at her sodden white coat. I carried her back into the bedroom and placed her softly on the bed. She was still breathing.

Matted blood covered her left ear as well as the right side of her head. Her right eye was swollen shut, and her left foreleg was broken. Using the flashlight, I carefully examined the wounds. The first one over the left ear looked like it had come from a well-placed kick. At eighteen, she no longer had any mobility to avoid one.

The second was probably from the barrel of his gun as she was lying helpless at his feet. Her left eye gazed up at me bravely from her trembling jaw.

I went into the bathroom and found a large towel. Ripping off a strip lengthwise, I took off my waterproof jacket and raised the bloody edge of the denim shirt above the two seeping holes in my side. Squeezing an inch of antibiotic ointment into each of them, I wrapped the towel tightly around my midsection, over-lapping it at the wounds. Holding the towel in place with my right hand, I went into the kitchen and found a roll of duct tape over the sink. I ran two lengths of it around my waist to hold the crude bandage in place. A million and one household uses.

Moistening the rest of the towel with tap water, I took it into the bedroom and lightly cleaned the wounds on Bug's face, covering each of them with the same antibiotic ointment. She never whimpered.

In the bathroom medicine chest, I found some Percodan tablets along with a bottle of Ambien I had once been prescribed. I popped two of the Percodan and palmed another along with the Ambien for Bug. With her ruined teeth, there was no way to sugarcoat the pain medicine with a chunk of raw steak. Gently sliding the pills into her throat, I made sure she swallowed them.

I had no idea if she would survive. There was a lot at stake, and I didn't think that taking her to a veterinarian at this point would make a difference. I hoped she would understand.

Her left eye was looking up at me with almost calm detachment, as if the danger had passed. I kissed her on her forehead and told her everything would be all right. My eyes blurred as I left.

I needed to search Sal's body. Lying in the lake water, his skin was already getting cold. I went through the zippered windbreaker he was wearing and found a cell phone in the side pocket.

Sal wasn't very smart. He had disabled the password requirement for his voice mailbox, and I went straight to it. He had saved Bobby Devane's last message, along with nine others dating back almost a month.

I recognized the voice immediately. It was the same one I had listened to back at the campus security office when I left the message for Devane earlier. He slowly gave Sal my address, repeating it twice. Then I heard his voice say, "You know what you told me you wanted to do? Go ahead, Sally, but don't fuck it up."

I had a pretty good idea what Sal Scalise had told him from the Wonderland. He had said it to me three times before I ever left the motel room. Unfortunately for him, he had fucked it up. Putting my waterproof jacket back on, I headed out into the storm.

21

The wind had become a living thing.

Heading across the high bluffs above Wiggins Point, I could barely keep the truck on the road against the sustained winds. Captain Morgo called me on the radio as I descended into the protection of the tree line that bordered the town.

"Anything new at your end?" she asked.

If I had possessed the energy, I would have laughed out loud.

I had already decided not to tell her about Sal Scalise. If I reported his death, Jim Dickey's investigators would have had me jumping through hoops for the rest of the day, if not longer. And time was running out.

If I stopped now, Jordan was finished at St. Andrews. And so was I, for that matter. Unless the cabin floated away, Sal wouldn't be going anywhere. And I was carrying his cell phone with the saved messages. I knew I could reconstruct what had happened when the time came. If things turned out all right, I could sleep for a week.

Captain Morgo had news for me.

"Ken found Creighton Taylor's old case file and was able to track down his college application documents in the college archives," she said.

"How did he die?" I asked. "It wasn't in the newspaper."

"He was found hanging from the suspension footbridge by a length of braided rope," she said.

"Multicolored, correct?"

"Yes," she confirmed, adding, "and his blood-alcohol level was incredibly high . . . point three seven."

"Anything else?"

"One odd thing. His right hand was inside the noose around his neck."

I could see it all in my mind.

"You also asked about his parents. As of June fifteenth, 1986, his mother was living in Fort Campbell, Kentucky. His father is listed on his college application as a major in the United States Army."

"Can you give me the father's full name?" I asked.

"Francis Marion Taylor. His home address is listed as Charlotte, South Carolina."

Francis Marion. The Swamp Fox of the Revolutionary War was from South Carolina, and he had been an incredible warrior. Along with ten thousand other Carolinians, Creighton Taylor's father had probably been named after him.

It was finally beginning to make sense. I asked Captain Morgo to make a call to the Pentagon and try to track down a lieutenant colonel named Mike Andrews who worked in operations planning.

212

"Will do," she said and cut the connection.

Less than ten minutes later, the office dispatcher patched me through to Andrews in Washington. By then, I was sitting in the middle of Triphammer Road, stopped in front of a downed tree that blocked the only route across the gorge onto the campus. Thankfully, the cell connection was still working.

"So what's the weather like up there in the boondocks?" asked Andrews. "You marooned at home in front of the fire with that feral white wolf?"

"I need a favor, Mike."

"Oh, shit," he came right back. "Here it comes again."

We had served together in Afghanistan. I hadn't saved his life. He hadn't saved mine. But we had hated the same brass idiots, and we had gotten drunk together over the time we fought there. And he knew I had gotten the shaft.

"I need everything you can find out pronto about an army officer named Francis Marion Taylor. He was a major in 1986 and probably served at some point with the 101st Airborne at Fort Campbell."

"You know how many goddamn Taylors have served in the army from old Zachary to Maxwell Taylor," he groaned. "Maybe fifty thousand."

"That's why I called you. He was probably born in South Carolina."

"Thanks a pantload. All right. Give me a couple weeks and I'll get back to you."

"You've got an hour. Call me back at the dispatcher's number and they'll patch me through . . . Mike . . . it could be life or death."

"Your life?"

"You never know."

"I'll do my best, Jake," he said, signing off.

Francis Marion Taylor. I was wondering where he might be at that moment when an emergency vehicle pulled up alongside me, and three men began removing cutting equipment from the freight bed.

I backed the Chevy to the side of the road and parked. While rain continued to pound the windshield, the emergency crew went to work on the tree. I fell asleep to the seductive whine of chainsaws dismantling the trunk.

Something slammed into the rear of the cab, bringing me up from the blackness. The Percodan had put me out. I blearily checked my watch. I had slept for about twenty minutes.

By now, the wind and rain should have moderated further unless the hurricane had slowed down or stopped in its path. I didn't see any hint of the storm abating. The sky was still dark as I started the truck up again. Through the windshield, I saw that the emergency crew had finished its work and moved on.

I needed to find Evelyn Wheatley. The last I had heard, she was riding out the storm at Tau Epsilon Rho with Mrs. Palmer. Swinging the Chevy around, I turned on the headlights again and headed over there.

22

Evelyn Wheatley was sitting next to an attractive blonde woman on one of the leather couches in the fraternity's chapter room. They were gazing out at the storm through the massive picture window. When she saw me coming, she stood up to face me.

I'm sure my physical appearance didn't inspire much confidence in my investigative capabilities. As I stood there dripping water on the floor, I saw the rage flaring in her eyes. It was obvious she had other issues on her mind.

"I placed my faith in you, Officer Cantrell," she spat bitterly, "and you allowed Robin to be murdered just like my husband. You are evidently just as incompetent as that idiot sheriff."

I noted that she hadn't included Hoyt Palmer among the dead.

"Due to the hurricane, the AuCoin agency is unable to fly in their investigative team," she went on, "but they'll arrive here as soon as the storm passes over us. In the meantime, why don't you go back to issuing parking tickets or harassing the students or whatever it is you do."

"That will probably be too late," I said.

"Too late for what?" she snapped back.

"To find and arrest your husband's killer."

The other woman hadn't risen from the couch. She was in her late twenties, at least seven or eight months pregnant, and looked Scandinavian, with blonde hair and blue eyes.

"Are you Mrs. Palmer?" I asked.

She nodded.

"I believe your husband is the key to finding out who is responsible for these deaths and why, Mrs. Palmer."

"I do not . . . speak English so very good," she said.

"I believe your husband is still alive, and I think you both know where he is," I said. "You have no reason to trust me at this point, but if I can talk to him right away, there's a chance I can find the killer in the next few hours."

"Trust you?" shouted Evelyn Wheatley in a mocking tone. "I would sooner trust the Pope to advocate for abortion."

She still hadn't bothered to deny that Hoyt Palmer was still alive.

"I'm convinced that this man plans to kill again," I said, "and the victim will almost certainly be your husband, Mrs. Palmer. I don't care how safely you think he's hidden, this man will find him and kill him . . . if not today then next week or next month."

"Frankly, we don't care a goddamn bit about what you're convinced of, Officer Cantrell," said Evelyn Wheatley. "Go now."

Her face had a new hardness to it, which was entirely understandable. I played the only card I had left.

"It's possible that the man who committed these murders will never be caught," I said. "These were revenge murders by someone who is unlikely to ever do it again. This could be the one chance we have to catch him and make him pay for what he has done."

"Revenge? Revenge for what?" she demanded.

"That's what Hoyt Palmer could tell us," I said.

Her eyes dropped to the floor. Looking down, I saw that a small rivulet of blood had trickled down the length of my loose waterproof pants. The red drops had pooled together to form a puddle on the parquet tile.

"I believe you're bleeding," she said in a tone she might have used if her butler was wearing a soiled tie over his morning coat.

"I was shot, Mrs. Wheatley."

That didn't seem to impress her much either. I wanted to add that I hadn't slept more than six hours over the last three nights, every muscle in my body was sore, I had a knife slash across my chest, my knuckles were barked and swollen, I had probably lost at least one tooth, my dog might be dying, and I had just killed a man.

"Was it in the course of investigating the murder of my husband?" she asked next.

I nodded back at her. Her hard brown eyes connected with mine and stayed there for several seconds. I don't know what made her change her mind. Maybe she needed to find out for herself if revenge was the motive for her husband's death, and if so, why. I'll never know for sure.

"All right . . . I'll take you to him." Turning to Mrs. Palmer, she added, "It'll be all right, Inge. Stay here and rest. I'll be back in a little while."

After retrieving a hooded slicker from her room, she joined me outside in the old pickup, pretending to ignore the coating of Bug fur that covered the passenger side of the seat.

As soon as we moved out from the protection of the covered entrance portico, the wind began buffeting the truck again as if we were inside a piñata. I was making my way around some fallen debris in the road when she said, "I knew that something was troubling Dennis. I assumed it had to do with a business matter. I never thought it might date back to something that happened in his college years."

A moment later, a spasm of grief hit her. She began to rock back and forth on the seat, her eyes tightly shut, her hands squeezed together in her lap.

"I'll be all right," she said huskily.

I decided not to tell her that her husband had pancreatic cancer or what I had learned about the murders. If he was still alive, Hoyt Palmer would fill in some of those answers. And she would believe them coming from him.

Opening her eyes again, she told me to drive to the college bell tower, which stood next to the library on the arts quadrangle. The bell tower housed the chimes that rang on the quarter hour.

I had been up in the tower only once, and that was as a student. As well as I could remember, it was about a hundred feet high. The bell chimes rested in wooden racks just below the clock in the belfry, each one controlled by a bell clapper from the room below. The chime masters could play everything from Mozart to the Beatles during their Sunday afternoon concerts.

Six inches of standing water covered the promenade between the library and the bell tower. I drove over the curb and parked on the grass next to the door that led to the iron staircase inside the tower. The solid oak door was locked, but I had a master key on my ring that opened most of the entry doors on the campus. It worked.

Inside, the noise of the wind was muted by the stone walls. I told Evelyn Wheatley to stay behind me, and we began to climb the steep narrow stairway. My joints and muscles were silently screaming at me, and I had to rest about halfway up, sitting down on one of the cold iron steps. Evelyn Wheatley glared at me with obvious impatience. I asked her if we were going up to the room where the chime masters operated the bells. She shook her head.

"Have you ever heard of the Plume and Dragon Society?" she asked.

"No," I grunted, standing up to resume the climb.

"It's made up of the most extraordinary students at St. Andrews. Dennis was a member. So was Hoyt Palmer. You can't ask to join it. The seniors in the society vote each spring on who will be tapped to carry on their sacred traditions. Its very existence is a secret from the rest of the student body."

I could imagine the sacred traditions. The new initiates bent over bare-assed while the rest of them used the sacred paddle. I was glad that no one had ever tapped me on the shoulder, but I wondered if Jordan Langford had been a member.

"They have a secret chamber up here," she said, starting to breathe as heavily as I was. "It's where Hoyt thought he would be safe until the murderer was caught."

The wind was whistling through hairline cracks in the mortared stone walls when we finally reached the landing below the chime masters' room. Evelyn Wheatley motioned for me to stop. Glancing around the landing, I saw no indication of a door or entryway in the stone facade.

She walked over to a heavy bronze lighting fixture that was mounted on the far wall. Rotating it to the side, she gripped the fixture in both hands and pulled hard on it. It must have been some kind of latch key, because a three-foot-square section of the lower wall suddenly slid open.

The door panel had a stone facade to match the rest of the wall. Its frame was made of wood and hinged on one side. We had to get down on our hands and knees to pass through the opening. I went first, carrying my flashlight in one hand and my cocked .45 in the other. Evelyn Wheatley shut the portal door behind us, and I heard it lock into the closed position.

Four candles were guttering on an elaborately carved table in the middle of the chamber. Against one of the walls, two stone gargoyles flanked an enormous upholstered throne chair.

A leather couch sat along another wall surrounded by leather club chairs and floor lamps, none of them lit.

Above our heads, heavy oak beams vaulted across the ceiling. A single leaded casement window provided the only natural light. It was too small for a man to climb through, even if he had scaled the hundred feet of stone to reach it. The room was cold and damp.

"Hoyt?" Mrs. Wheatley's voice rang out.

On the other side of the room, a heavy oak door led into a second chamber. The door stood ajar, but there was no light coming from beyond it. I shined my flashlight into the room. It was smaller than the main chamber and contained a clothing rack holding Druid-like blue velvet cloaks.

I heard a sudden movement and shined my flashlight toward it. The beam found Palmer cowering on his knees behind the clothing rack.

"Why did you bring him here?" he whispered angrily. "You promised not to tell anyone, Evelyn."

As he came toward us, I saw that he was still dressed in his green medical center pajamas and bathrobe.

"I thought it best," she said.

Palmer had the beach-boy looks of an aging surfer, with a thick helmet of grayish-blond hair and blue eyes like his wife.

"Officer Cantrell has promised to protect you, Hoyt," she said.

"No one can protect me," he groaned. "He'll find me no matter where I go."

"Who will find you?" she asked.

"I don't know," he said. "It's over the boy."

"What boy?" she demanded. "What are you talking about?"

Palmer plodded in his slippers back into the first chamber, heading straight toward the burning candelabra like a moth seeking the flame. We followed after him, and I eased myself into one of the club chairs.

"How did you get past the policeman at the hospital?" I asked.

He forced a nervous grin at me.

"I was hiding in one of the other rooms when the two of you went to check on me. I waited for you to go past before I took off. Evelyn and Inge were waiting for me in the parking lot. That's when I decided to head—"

"What did you mean about the boy?" interrupted Evelyn Wheatley. "I must know."

Before he could respond, the bells above us suddenly started to toll.

"Oh, God," Palmer cried out. "He's up there . . . he's coming for me."

I looked at my watch. It was exactly one o'clock.

"The electricity must have been restored. The chimes are set to play automatically," I said as they tolled.

My words didn't erase the look of terror in his face. His fear was like a tangible thing in the room with us, abetted by the constant moan of the wind outside the stone walls.

"I don't want to die," he said. "I'm not a brave man, Evelyn."

"Die for what?" she asked harshly. "Pull yourself together and tell me what you did."

Hearing the tone of rebuke in her voice, he took in a deep breath. Running his hands through his blond hair, he said, "I . . . I'm not proud of what I'm about to tell you. I've spent my life trying to atone for it."

"Just like Wheatley and Massey," I said.

He nodded at me.

I suddenly felt the hair prickling up on the back of my neck. It was my extra sense checking in again. Pulling out my radio, I called Captain Morgo. She responded immediately. I told her that we had found Hoyt Palmer and exactly where we were. I asked her to send over at least three officers to protect the tower building until an escort could be arranged to take him to a secure place.

She told me that aside from Ken Macready and her two dispatchers, everyone was now deployed on the campus. She promised to send Ken right over and said she would call the sheriff's office and ask that two deputies be dispatched immediately to escort Palmer back to the campus police building.

Evelyn Wheatley waited until I had turned off the radio again before saying, "Tell me about this boy right now, Hoyt."

Turning to me with a grisly attempt at a smile, he said, "Did you join a fraternity in college?"

I shook my head no.

"Do you know what a closet case is?" he asked.

"Everyone knows what a closet case is," snapped Mrs. Wheatley. "Get on with it."

"Well . . . during our junior year, there was a bad drinking incident at Tau Epsilon Rho. Two girls were sent to the hospital, and we almost lost our charter over it. The following year, we were on probation . . . and our pledge class really suffered. We had to take guys who ordinarily would have been blackballed . . . you must know what I mean."

I nodded again to keep him talking.

"Anyway, this one kid had showed up the first night with the rest of the herd . . . he was fat . . . and really clumsy. From the moment he arrived, he began bumping into furniture, knocking things over, spilling the punch . . . wherever he went, something happened. Another thing was that he couldn't keep our names straight. He would call me Robin and he would call Robin Dennis. Maybe he was dyslexic . . . we didn't know what dyslexia was in those days . . . he just seemed as dumb as a post. He would have been blackballed any other year, but because of the probation situation, the brothers ended up taking him."

"Many men are clumsy," said Evelyn Wheatley. "Dennis was clumsy."

Palmer began to gnaw at the knuckle of his right thumb. I saw a spot of blood where his teeth had bitten hard. His eyes slowly became riveted on it.

"Hoyt," barked Evelyn Wheatley.

"I . . . I was the one assigned to go to his room and tell him the good news," he said, now unable to look at her. "When he opened the door and saw me standing there, he started beaming at me like it was Christmas morning. On the way back to the fraternity, he kept telling me it was the greatest thing to happen in his life."

"But he didn't live happily ever after," I said.

"Looking back, I guess he wasn't really a closet case . . . he was just a big gentle bear of a kid," said Palmer, as if trying to make belated amends. "We started calling him Oaf. That became his pledge name. I don't know . . . I guess some of the brothers hoped he would quit."

He paused to look across at me again. It was obvious he was one of them.

"My mouth is very dry," he said huskily, pointing at a bottle of water on the sideboard next to the table.

I reached over and grabbed the bottle, passing it across to him. He took several swallows. When he put it down, his hands were shaking. Evelyn Wheatley looked away.

"Eventually, even the other pledges didn't want to have anything to do with him," he said. "He was like that cartoon character who always had the rain clouds over his head. The brothers made him the butt of most of the hazing stunts. He always got the dirtiest pledge assignments."

The brothers, I thought, shaking my head in disgust.

"But no matter what we did to him, he seemed to take it in stride. It was crazy. I mean, he was a big guy . . . like in *Of Mice and Men*. He was so naïve that he never even knew we were tormenting him. I guess it was actually kind of endearing in a way . . . but of course, we never saw it like that at the time. So he came in for even more special attention."

His lips were barely moving when he said, "I regret to say we did all kinds of things to him."

"What things?" demanded Evelyn Wheatley.

"You don't want to know," he said, shaking his head. "But Creighton went along with it all like it was part of the wonderful bonding process you went through to become our brother."

It was the first time he had used the boy's name.

"On pledge night, someone . . . I think it was Dennis . . . came up with an idea to make him quit. While the other pledges were all gathered down in the chapter room, we took him up to our suite on the top floor."

"Who took him?" I asked.

"Dennis . . . and Robin . . . and me," he said, his voice trailing off to barely a whisper.

"It started with a bottle of whiskey. There was about half a bottle left. We told him to chug the whole thing. All the other pledges were still celebrating down in the chapter room when we led him outside and over to the bridge."

I could see it all in my mind's eye.

"He was having trouble walking straight," went on Palmer. "Dennis had brought a length of stout cord with him that he had found in the chapter room. It was braided with a lot of colors and was used on ceremonial occasions. He tied one end loosely around Creighton's waist and the other end around one of the bridge stanchions. Then someone said, 'It's time for you to walk the line, Oaf.'"

It was obvious from the pathetic expression on Palmer's face that he had been the one.

"Even as drunk as he was, Creighton started to shake. He looked at the three of us in turn and said, 'Please don't. I'm really afraid of heights.'

"'A big guy like you?' someone shouted back at him."

Palmer's voice caught in his throat, and he had to pause again. Tears appeared in his eyes, and he didn't bother to wipe them away.

"Truly . . . none of us expected him to get up there. We thought he would chicken out, and then we would tell him he didn't pass muster to join the fraternity . . . And then he actually climbed up on the railing. 'Walk the line, Oaf, and you can be our brother,' someone shouted up at him. But he didn't . . . he was just like . . . paralyzed . . . he kept his arms rigidly at his sides . . . like he was standing at attention."

Evelyn Wheatley was staring at him with absolute scorn in her eyes.

"And then what?" she demanded.

"He . . . he was actually sobbing . . . and then, oh, God . . . and then . . . he went over."

It was almost exactly as I had pictured it.

"We . . . we all thought he would be saved by the rope Dennis had tied around him, but the rope was loosely tied . . . it just swept up over his shoulders. At the last second, he managed to get one hand inside the rope as it pulled tight around his neck . . . but it was . . . too late."

He was staring at his bloody knuckle again.

He let out a long sigh and said, "When we pulled him back up, he was dead . . . his neck had been broken."

As if almost dreading what he would see, Palmer turned to look at Evelyn Wheatley again, his shoulders slumped.

"And you just left him there like that?" she asked, her voice full of contempt.

She seemed to ignore the fact that her husband and Massey had been fellow conspirators.

"Jake," I heard someone yell out from the stairwell, and Palmer bolted upright. I recognized Ken Macready's voice. Going to the hidden passageway, I found the mechanism to slide the portal open.

Ken was standing there, his parka covered with mud. He looked a lot more self-assured since I had last seen him. He had obviously come through the storm a better officer.

"You look like hell, Jake," he said, staring at my bloodstained waterproofs. "Do you need to go to the hospital?"

"I was already there," I said, asking him to remain in the stairwell and to be prepared for a possible intruder. As I went back inside, Ken drew his Glock 17 and checked it to make sure there was a round in the chamber.

"Evelyn, we spent our lives atoning for it," Palmer pleaded in a beseeching tone.

"How did Taylor's father find out the truth?" I asked him.

"It's his father?" asked Palmer.

"I think so."

"I have no idea," he said. "Only the three of us knew what happened, and none of us has ever breathed a word of it."

He looked over at Evelyn Wheatley, his eyes silently begging for forgiveness. Without another word, she stood up and left the secret chamber.

Palmer stared down at his hands again and began to sob.

23

While standing with Ken in the stairwell, I called Captain Morgo on the radio and told her that the man who had killed Wheatley and Robin Massey was almost certainly the father of Creighton Taylor. She said she would call the sheriff's office right away so they could swear out a warrant for his arrest as a material witness in the case.

Ten minutes later, Jim Dickey's two deputies arrived. Ken and I waited for them on the landing outside the chamber. The first one came bounding up the staircase two steps at a time. He wasn't even breathing heavily when he joined us outside the passageway. The deputy was young and black with an open, intelligent face.

"The cavalry has arrived," he said with a grin.

The second man lagged about forty feet behind him. When he finally huffed and puffed his way up to the landing, I saw he had a large paunch protruding through the open rain jacket over his uniform. The nameplate on his breast pocket read, "Dickey." He was Big Jim's older brother, Darryl.

"The sheriff has decided to question this man Hoyt personally," he said. "He wants him kept right here."

Big Jim obviously saw an opportunity to become the hero in a high-profile murder investigation. He didn't want the principal witness exposed until he could bring him in with appropriate fanfare.

"I think we should get him back to a secure place as quickly as possible," I said. "The man stalking him is—"

"I already told you. The sheriff wants him kept right here," he repeated as if it were an imperial decree. In a way, it was. Once the missing persons alert for Hoyt Palmer had gone out, the sheriff was technically in charge of the case. I didn't say anything further.

"So what's his problem?" he asked as Palmer continued to sob uncontrollably inside the chamber.

I told him.

"And the man who may have murdered his two friends is ex-army airborne," I added. "He probably had Special Forces training. If I were you, I wouldn't wait until the sheriff arrives to get the witness out of here."

He grinned back at me and said, "Son, I been huntin' since I was five years old. I know how to stalk wild game as well as anybody, so don't you worry now." Turning to the black deputy, he said, "Marlon, you head back downstairs and guard the door. It's the only way up. I'll stay here."

I pulled Ken aside and told him not to leave Palmer alone for any reason until he was back in protective custody at either the sheriff's office or the campus security police building.

"Don't worry, Jake," he said.

Evelyn Wheatley was waiting for me when I got to the foot of the iron staircase.

The young black deputy was standing behind her in the stairwell next to the massive oak door. He forced the door open against the strength of the wind and held it for us until we went out. I heard it close behind us.

I had forgotten to turn off the truck's headlights, and the engine barely turned over before it finally caught. Putting the transmission into first gear, I headed across the storm-ravaged campus one more time.

Evelyn Wheatley didn't say a word on the ride back. When we arrived at the covered entrance of her husband's fraternity house, she made no move to get out of the truck. Almost a minute passed while she sat quietly and stared out at the rain.

"I felt such . . . such helpless anger as I listened to him," she said finally. "And Dennis . . . he . . . he—"

"Your husband spent his life trying to atone for it," I said, interrupting her. "Try to always remember that."

Maybe the knowledge of what her husband did with Massey and Palmer had somehow released her from a lifelong obligation. When she turned to look at me, all the rage had drained out of her face. It looked delicate again.

"I will never come back here," she said softly.

I went around and opened the passenger door for her. She stepped down from the cab, and I watched her walk across the entryway until she disappeared through the front door.

24

According to my watch, it was almost one thirty. I wondered if Bobby Devane or Brian Razzano had tried to reach me. Turning on the transceiver again, I checked with the dispatcher to find out whether I had any phone messages. Carlene was on duty and said that no calls had come in for me.

As I pulled into the parking lot behind the police building, a sheet of wood paneling flew past the windshield as if it was a piece of stationery. Before I could get out of the truck, Carlene called me back to say that an army officer was trying to reach me from Washington. I asked her to patch him through. It was Mike Andrews.

"Well, I tracked your man down," he said. "It wasn't as hard as I thought. He was no ticket puncher, Jake. The guy was one hell of a combat soldier, although he didn't do so well later in the Pentagon under the eyes of the almighty brass. I guess he didn't like ass-kissing as much as soldiering. Anyway, he made it to brigade command before they finally retired him."

So Taylor had gotten his star. He had made brigadier general.

"A retired sergeant major I trust told me that Frank Taylor was one of the best battalion commanders in Vietnam during that whole goddam war."

"Did he serve with the 101st?"

"Yeah . . . he was leading a company when the 101st relieved Hue after Tet. He won a Silver Star at Perfume River . . . and later on another one near Pleiku."

"What regiment was he with?" I asked.

I could hear him flipping the pages of a personnel file before he said, "The five oh deuce."

Ben Massengale hadn't been so drunk after all. He had gotten it right.

"Mike, you only owe me sixteen more favors," I said.

"The next time you're in Washington, just take me to the Palm for lunch," he came back. "I'll order the twenty-four-ounce prime rib."

"Sure," I said, signing off.

So where are you now, General Taylor? I wondered.

The squad room was mobbed as I came through the rear door and headed straight for the emergency medical technician who was sitting on one of the cots in the hallway. She looked as exhausted as I felt. I asked her to bring her medical kit to my cubicle. Taking off my waterproof jacket, I pulled up the lower edge of the bloody denim shirt and asked her to put a new bandage on the wounds.

"Duct tape," she laughed.

She sliced the tape with medical scissors and gently pulled the ends away from the towel I had used for a bandage. The entrance and exit wounds looked like the puckered mouths of two trout.

"This looks like a bullet wound," she said, glancing up at me.

"I was speared by a length of copper tubing. Just take care of it."

She looked back up at me dubiously before spraying anesthetic on the holes and taping on a new bandage.

There was no doubt in my mind that General Taylor was within a few hundred yards of where I was now sitting. He wasn't about to leave. Not when he had one more job to do.

I tried to put myself in Taylor's position when he had first arrived at St. Andrews a couple of nights earlier. He had probably never visited the campus. Thirty years ago, he might well have been deployed overseas. His son was here for only five months.

I thought about where I would have chosen to stay in a strange town where my son's life had ended so long ago. I would have stayed in the same place my son had lived during the months he was here as a student. The last place he had lived before his death.

Captain Morgo walked in on us a moment later and saw the bandage covering my side.

"How bad is it, Jake?"

"I've had worse," I said, putting on the waterproof jacket to cover it.

Before she had a chance to ask what had happened to me, I gave her the details of my interview with Hoyt Palmer. After telling her about General Taylor, I suddenly remembered Palmer saying that he had been the fraternity brother assigned to visit Creighton Taylor on the night he had been tapped to become one of their anointed pledges.

"Could you get Ken on the VHF and ask him to find out from Palmer where Creighton Taylor was living when he visited him on pledge night?" I asked her.

While she tried to reach Ken on the radio, I trudged into the lavatory and took a long, satisfying leak. When I came back out to the squad room, she was still trying. After another unsuccessful attempt, she said, "There must be some malfunction with his radio. I can't raise him."

I called Lauren Kenniston again.

"Does the story in the *Journal* say where Creighton Taylor was living at the start of his freshman year here?" I asked.

"Let me check," she said.

"Drink this," ordered Captain Morgo, handing me a large plastic cup she had just carried over from the refreshment bar.

I took a sip. It was a thick chocolate milkshake and was as delicious as anything I had ever tasted. I finished it as Lauren came back on the phone.

"His last known local mailing address was 326 Highland Drive."

Highland Drive was the first cross street after the traffic bridge. It led down to the Fall Creek Tavern. I didn't know the street numbers, but there were a lot of homes on that street where people rented rooms to students.

Captain Morgo said she would drive me over in her cruiser. Outside, the rain was finally losing its intensity. The wind wasn't quite so violent either, but it was still gusting fiercely enough to make the trees on campus sway wildly before its might.

We had just crossed the traffic bridge over the gorge when Captain Morgo received a call on her cell phone. She listened for almost a minute before saying, "Stay there. I'll call you right back."

She turned to me and said, "That was Ken Macready. Hoyt Palmer is dead."

25

I could have prevented Palmer's death if I had been more
forceful in demanding that he be moved out of the tower
right away. In some subconscious way, maybe I had wanted it
to happen.

We got there in less than two minutes. Two of the sheriff's
cars were parked outside the tower, their strobe lights flashing.
One of them was Dickey's blue-and-gold cruiser. It was empty.
The oak door at the base of the tower stood wide open. The black
deputy was no longer there guarding it.

I wasn't thrilled about climbing that iron staircase again but
managed to follow Captain Morgo all the way to the top without stopping. Ken Macready was standing on the same landing
where I had left him.

"You're not going to believe this," he said, pointing through
the dark passageway into the secret chamber. Ken's uniform hat
was missing, and the hair on the back of his head was stained
with blood.

"I never even saw him. It was like fighting a ghost."

"What happened to your radio?" asked Captain Morgo.

"He took it, Captain," he said sheepishly. "Along with the sheriff's radio and his brother's too. And all our weapons. As soon as I saw what was in there, I called you on my cell . . . he didn't find that," he added almost proudly.

Ken was still holding the phone in his hand. After checking to make sure the wound to the back of his head wasn't serious, I followed Captain Morgo on our hands and knees through the passageway into the chamber.

Ken was right. It was hard to believe the scene that awaited us. High above our heads, Hoyt Palmer was hanging by his neck from the same kind of multicolored rope that had been used in the two previous murders.

His body was slowly swinging back and forth under one of the hand-hewn oak beams that vaulted over the chamber walls. The other end of the braided rope was lashed to the nose of one of the stone gargoyles that flanked the throne chair against the outer wall.

Even more incredible was the sight of Big Jim Dickey and his brother. The two men were splayed out on their knees facing one another, about three feet apart. Taylor had taken their handcuffs and shackled the brothers' wrists together through the arms of the throne chair. They looked as though they were kneeling before an absent king.

Turning to Ken, Captain Morgo asked, "How did all this happen?"

"He took our keys, goddammit," said Big Jim from down on his knees. "Call my brother Cecil and ask him to get over here right away with bolt cutters."

"We've got an emergency crew that can bring them over from the campus police building in a few minutes," said Janet Morgo.

"Call Cecil, goddammit," he growled, obviously worried that his monumental incompetence would be exposed to the voters if the campus emergency crew arrived first.

"Give me your cell phone, Ken," I said, punching the number Dickey called out to me from the floor. While it was ringing, I began taking pictures of Palmer's hanging corpse. I framed Big Jim and his brother prominently in the foreground.

"What the hell are you doing, Cantrell?" yelled the sheriff, trying to turn around from his locked embrace. His brother appeared to be resting his face on the arm of the throne chair.

"Just recording a crime scene, Sheriff, like any good cop would do," I said good-naturedly. "And Cecil isn't picking up."

Cutting off the connection, I punched in Lauren Kenniston's number and sent her a text to come immediately to the bell tower. Her first exclusive. I followed up with a call to the dispatcher's number at the campus police building. Carlene answered immediately. I told her to send an emergency rescue team to the tower with bolt cutters.

I then placed a 9-1-1 call, which went straight to the sheriff's office. After identifying myself, I told the dispatcher there that another murder had been committed at the bell tower on the

St. Andrews campus and to send over their homicide team. I knew Lauren would be monitoring it on her scanner.

"Sheriff Dickey is in a bit of a bind," I said. "Tell them to hurry."

"You fucking bastard . . . I'll run you out of Groton for this."

I took more photographs.

"I don't want you threatening one of my men, Sheriff," came back Janet Morgo. "Officer Cantrell is only doing his job."

"And I'll have your job, too, you goddamn bull dyke," he snarled up at her.

Ignoring him, Captain Morgo turned to Ken and said, "So tell us what happened here."

He was obviously still woozy and sat down in one of the leather club chairs.

"When the sheriff got here, he told Marlon, the deputy guarding the entrance at the bottom of the stairs, to go back on sector duty . . . that he would handle things here himself," he said. "He then told me to stay out on the landing while he and his brother questioned Mr. Palmer. A few minutes later, the chimes started ringing up in the tower like there was no tomorrow."

"And the sheriff sent you up there to take a look, right?" I said.

"Yes, sir," said Ken. "When I got to the top of the stairwell, the emergency lights suddenly went out. I felt a blow to the back of my head . . . I guess it put me down for a while. When I came to, the lights were back on. There was no one up in the belfry, so I went back down the stairs and looked in here. It was just like you saw it. That's when I called Captain Morgo."

So Taylor had closed the last account.

"How could one man have done all this?" whispered Captain Morgo in my ear.

"Special Forces training," I said. "Taylor may be an old man, but taking Dickey and his brother in the dark would have been child's play for him."

I walked back to the throne chair.

"I warned your brother about this possibility, Sheriff," I said. "You may be in for a long vacation after this gets out."

This time he stayed silent, his steer-like arms and back rippling under his uniform shirt, his face a mottled red. Motioning Captain Morgo to join me in the stairwell, I reminded her that we had a possible address for General Taylor if he hadn't already left Groton.

We passed the St. Andrews emergency crew coming up the stairs. They were carrying two heavy vinyl bags full of rescue equipment. Following in their wake was Lauren Kenniston, who gave me a big smile as she came hustling up the staircase. I was expecting Captain Morgo to tell her that the crime scene was off-limits to the news media, but she never said a word as Lauren passed us.

Back in the cruiser, she didn't say anything for several minutes. When we had crossed over the bridge and reached the intersection that connected to Highland Drive, she turned to me with liquid eyes and asked, "What does my being a lesbian have to do with whether I can do my job?"

"Nothing," I said.

26

The rain had finally stopped, although the sky remained a dense charcoal gray. I was noting the street numbers on Highland Drive as we drove slowly past the rooming houses. All the lawns were covered with branches and storm debris.

"It has to be on the next block," I said.

As we approached the cross street, Captain Morgo said, "Oh, my lord," and pulled the cruiser to the side of the road. Farther down the windswept plateau, the Fall Creek Tavern was lit up like a Hollywood movie set.

Two Groton police cruisers bracketed the street at the top of the steep grade. A red fire truck sat on the road below them, its mounted floodlights trained toward the building.

Going forward on foot, we saw that the Groton police had cordoned off the area near the gorge. More than a hundred people were standing behind the police lines on the other side of the road.

In the glare of the floodlights, I could see that the bar was empty. Many of the bystanders had managed to save some of the liquor stock before being evacuated and were making short work of it while they watched the rest of the drama unfold.

The building no longer rested on its original foundation. It had slid back toward the gorge, and the whole building was now slightly canted over the two-hundred-foot abyss.

Six Groton police officers guarded the perimeter of the cordoned-off area. As we came up, one of them recognized Captain Morgo and waved us past the rope barricade. A man in khaki overalls was standing near the front entrance of the building next to a Groton police lieutenant.

"It could go any minute," he was saying to the police officer. "There's nothing left to support it in the back . . . and when the rear half goes, it will take the rest of the building with it."

Walking around the side of the building, I looked out over the precipice and saw that the timbers and cross struts that had shored up the rear half of the building were completely gone. A few hung loose from the floor joists, suspended over the edge like stick figures. The side door to the bar was slamming back and forth with each wind gust. That was when I saw the hand-painted numbers above the doorway. I had never noticed them before that moment.

"326," the numbers read.

So Creighton Taylor had lived in one of the upstairs rooms at the Creeker. I looked up at the top tier of windows. They were all dark. I wondered if General Taylor might be up there if he had stayed in his son's room.

I could see the corner of one of the pool tables poking through a smashed window in the rear half of the building, ready to break loose. There was a deep, grinding rumble, followed by the loud snap of boards cracking and the sound of shattering glass. The building appeared to shudder for several seconds and then began to slowly travel downhill.

A roar went up from the crowd. It faded away as the foundation timbers ground to a halt. Someone in the crowd began singing in a ragged voice, "*The night they drove old Creeker down.*" It was Johnny Joe Splendorio, obviously too far gone to realize that the central focus of his existence was about to disappear.

I saw the owner, Chuck McKinlay, standing at the edge of the crowd. He was holding an unopened bottle of Banfi Brunello in his left hand and a full decanter of his prized Napoleon brandy in his right. Tears were streaming down his face as I went over to him.

"I need your help, Chuck," I said.

He seemed to be in a trance, or more likely drunk. His head slowly craned upward until our eyes met.

"Oh, hi, Jake," he said.

"Did you rent one of your upstairs rooms within the last few days to a man who wanted it for homecoming weekend?"

He reacted as if I had asked him to explain the theory of relativity.

"I mean . . . tell me, Jake . . . how did you know the tavern was going to die?"

I shook him by the shoulders.

Both bottles fell from his hands and smashed on the pavement.

"Oh, God," he cried. "My Brunello."

I repeated my question, my face a few inches from his.

"The room for the weekend . . . oh, yeah . . . the guy who wanted the attic space on the fifth floor."

"What happened to him?" I demanded.

"Dunno."

I found Captain Morgo again at the edge of the police barricade.

"I think our killer is upstairs in the tavern," I said. "I'm going in there to find out."

"Don't be crazy. It could go any second now."

"If I don't make it out in time, I want you to know there is a dead man named Sal Scalise lying in the kitchen of my cottage out at the lake. I killed him this afternoon after he tried to murder me. The reasons can be found in a batch of recorded messages on his cell phone that I have locked in my desk back at the office."

She shook her head with disbelief.

"He also tried to kill my dog, and she may still be alive. I'm asking you to send someone out there to take her to a vet as quickly as possible."

I could still see the uncertainty in her eyes.

"Trust me," I said with a weary grin.

"I do trust you, Jake. I was wrong about you, and I'm sorry."

I gave her a kiss on the cheek and began jogging toward the side entrance of the building.

"Where the hell is he going?" I heard the Groton police lieutenant shout as I went through the open doorway.

27

As soon as I stepped inside, the walls began to convulse, which generated another roar from the crowd across the road. Crossing the buckled floor, I went straight up the backstairs behind the kitchen, following the frayed carpet runner.

The wind was moaning through the broken windows on the fourth floor. Halfway down the hallway, another narrow staircase abutted the chimney. It led up into the darkness of the attic on the fifth floor. I turned on my flashlight and headed up.

The attic was choked with discarded mattresses, furniture, and wooden packing crates. Under the open rafters, the gusting wind sounded like the breathing of some primordial beast. Pigeon droppings and plaster dust swirled around me, creating a murky, sour fog.

Since Afghanistan, I had never felt I had knowingly experienced post-traumatic stress syndrome until that very moment. In my mind's eye, I saw the faces of the men I had lost, the horrific ruin of them after the Taliban had finished with them. For a few seconds, I couldn't move as I stood in the murky fog and tried to wipe out the memory.

I felt the building suddenly shift again. Off balance, I grabbed the nearest doorjamb and held on. When the grinding noise stopped, I saw a faint gleam of light spilling out of one of the doorways.

Hearing a low burst of chatter on my radio, I reached into my jacket pocket and turned it off. Pulling my .45 out of its shoulder holster, I moved slowly forward along the plaster wall until I could see into the room.

In the far corner, an old Coleman kerosene lantern sat on a metal desk. A .45 semiautomatic exactly like mine rested alongside it. Next to the gun was a framed photograph of a young man.

I stepped into the room.

"You won't need that," said Francis Marion Taylor, looking straight into the barrel of my pistol.

The expression on his lean and weathered face was as tranquil as if he had just enjoyed a good steak dinner and was waiting for bedtime. There were deeply grooved wrinkles around his pale-gray eyes. I recognized him immediately.

He had been sitting next to Ben at the bar when the four slumming angels had asked about Guadalcanal. He was wearing the same army field jacket with the Vietnam combat badge.

"So you have finally brought me to bay, Major Cantrell," he said with a taut grin.

I dropped the .45 to my side as a loud vibration began to shake the outer wall beneath the rafters. It sounded like a professional boxer working a light bag.

"I'm not sure how long this building is going to last," said General Taylor. "You should find a safe exit while you can."

"I take it you're not planning to go with me."

"No."

I doubted I could take him against his will and decided to play for time, if there was any time left, before the building went.

"I needed to ask you why," I said, holstering my .45. "I think I already know the answer."

"When Creighton died, I was deployed in Bolivia with a covert antidrug task force that was then assisting their government. By the time I returned home, he had been buried, both literally and figuratively. One of the boys in the fraternity he had just pledged had told police that he was depressed over breaking up with his girlfriend. The district attorney determined it was a suicide and ended their official inquiry."

"Who was the fraternity boy?" I asked.

"Dennis Wheatley."

"Yes," I said.

"I knew that Creighton hadn't been there long enough to have a girlfriend. He was so naïve in many ways. I suspected that there was more to it, but my wife begged me not to let my anger over his loss consume me . . . and to move on with our lives. Then the Persian Gulf heated up, and I was deployed there for two years followed by the invasion of Panama. I was overseas for pretty much the next five years. Then my wife died. The years passed. Creighton became a distant and painful memory, one that I simply wanted to avoid."

A crack of splintering wood was followed by another building shift. I watched as the Coleman lantern slowly slid off the edge of the metal desk and rolled down the canted floor.

"What happened to make you change your mind?"

"Earlier this year, I received a letter from an officer who had served under me in Iraq and was now in charge of the ROTC program here at St. Andrews. He asked if I was aware that a chair was being endowed at the new nanoscience learning center in the name of Creighton Taylor. He wondered if I planned to be on hand for the inaugural lecture. I told him that no one from the school had contacted me to let me know."

I nodded in anticipation of his next words.

"Considering Creighton had been a new transfer student when he died, it made no sense that he would have a chair named in his honor unless there was another reason for it."

"Guilt," I said.

He nodded back.

It was Wheatley's own money that caused his murder, just as his money had to be behind the blackmail threat.

"It wasn't easy, but I found out that this chair was one of several endowments underwritten by the Wheatley Foundation. That's when I decided to come back here to meet him and find out what really happened to Creighton."

"You still had doubts?"

He nodded and said, "Right up until Wheatley confessed just before I helped him up on the railing," he said. "He told me it was the three of them—him, Massey, and Palmer."

I stared at him in sadness.

"Grief and rage," he said. "Two very powerful forces . . . as powerful as that hurricane out there . . . powerful enough to choke off every other human emotion. I did try to fight it. My late wife would never have countenanced this."

The building convulsed for another ten seconds, and then it was quiet again.

"It was like finding out I had incurable cancer."

"And now you're cured."

"Hardly," he said, picking up the framed photograph from the desk and tossing it over to me.

"Creighton was my blood," he continued as I looked down at his son's broad, innocent face. "The last of my family there will ever be. I wonder if you can understand that."

"Nobody wrote a rulebook for something like this."

"Like most of my ancestors, I wanted to be a warrior. It took me away from my family during most of the years Creighton was growing up. In many ways, I've led a wasted life."

"I would have liked a mulligan myself."

He smiled. He had a good smile.

"I've got a different future planned now."

I knew what he meant to do. I kept wondering how I could get us both out of there alive. I didn't want his death on my conscience to go along with the other three in Afghanistan. I handed the photograph of his son back to him. He placed it on the table next to his .45.

"Why did you make Massey . . . ?"

"He wanted to go out naked," he said, already knowing where I was heading with the question. "Don't ask me why."

"Guilt makes people do strange things."

"I'm told you were a good army officer," said Taylor next.

"By whom?"

"I checked you out with friends at Fort Benning after Ben Massengale told me what happened to you in Afghanistan. The army makes mistakes."

"Yeah . . . I learned that," I said.

"You weren't responsible for the deaths of those men. You were betrayed by a border chieftain who was supposed to be our ally."

"And he wasn't punished for it," I said bitterly. "The general in command gave him a free pass."

"They circled the wagons. Generals are more important than majors. I guess you learned that too."

"The faces of those men have haunted me ever since."

"They never leave you."

"I checked you out too, General," I said.

"Really."

"My friend told me you could have had one of the top slots in the corporation, but you didn't take to the rarified atmosphere of the Pentagon."

"Or it didn't take to me. Either way, it wasn't a good fit."

His gray eyes were so luminously pale that they looked lit from inside. They followed me as I walked over to the shattered window and glanced out.

I wondered what our chances of survival would be if we jumped from there. A big sycamore tree was waving its branches about fifty feet away. There was no way to reach it unless I could fly. Glancing back at General Taylor, it was obvious he knew exactly what I was thinking. He watched me intently as I came back toward him.

"After telling me what they had done to my boy, do you know what Wheatley said? He said he would create a ten-million-dollar memorial scholarship in Creighton's name here at the college . . . and he was going to pay me a substantial annuity for everything my family had suffered. He offered me money."

"He was just trying to make up for what they had done in the only way he knew how," I said.

His eyes went cold again.

"Are you a father?" he asked.

I shook my head.

"Well, I hope you never have to find out what it's like to lose your only child, my friend."

I was about to tell him that Wheatley had pancreatic cancer and would have been dead in a few weeks when the building tremors began again a moment later. I felt them first in my feet. It was as if I was standing too close to the railroad tracks and a big freight was rumbling past.

"We have to go now, General," I said, keeping my voice calm.

"So go, Major."

"Not without you."

"Everybody dies."

"In due time."

"There's no reason for both of us to end our lives here, Jake."

"I'm not leaving without you, General," I said, taking a step toward him.

"You apparently need further encouragement," he said, as if I were an obstinate pupil. Sweeping the .45 up from the desk, he thumbed back the hammer. I stopped short. He paused again to look down at his son's face.

Grabbing the framed photograph of his son, he hugged it to his chest with his left hand, swung the .45 away from me, pointed it at his heart, and pulled the trigger.

28

staggered through the dark attic back to the narrow enclosed staircase by the chimney. My first thought was to try to get to the third floor. From there, I could jump from one of the windows and probably survive.

I was a few yards from the head of the staircase when the chimney suddenly disintegrated and the stairs collapsed. The only way out of the fifth-floor attic now was through the shattered window in the general's room.

It sounded like a wrecking ball was hammering the remaining building supports as I retraced my path. The floor joists were shaking like they were about to come apart, and the front of the building started to angle upward before taking its final plunge.

The general's body was sliding down the canted floor when I reached the doorway to his room. Through the window, I could see that the upper floors were already well out over the precipice, a good ten feet beyond the edge. Two hundred feet below, rain-swollen black water raced down the chasm.

On the far side of the gorge, a small cluster of people had gathered on the cliff trail, waiting to witness the final act. One of them must have seen me in the window because she began excitedly pointing me out to the others.

I decided to take my chances from the window. About fifty feet below me, I saw a shale ledge extending out about five feet from the rest of the gorge. There was a chance I could swing from the edge of the window frame far enough back toward the face to reach it when I fell. Then I would just have to avoid the building falling on top of me. It seemed like the best of my limited options.

I was about to swing my right leg out the window when there was a loud rending screech, and the section of roof above my head ripped free from the wall joists and hurtled away into the gorge.

Crouching down against the force of the wind, my left hand brushed the transceiver in my side pocket. *You stupid asshole*, I thought. I had turned the radio off before approaching the general's lair and had forgotten about it. Turning it on, I immediately heard Janet Morgo's voice.

". . . to the front side of the building," came her voice, calmly and clearly. "If you can hear me, Jake, come to the front side of the attic."

She kept repeating the same words as I began making my way back along the tilting hallway. The attic floor was crammed with shifting junk, and it was slow going as I climbed over each obstruction. With a great tearing sound, another section of the roof ripped away, and I could see the murky gray sky directly above me.

I had waited too long. This was the end of the line.

There was a final rending screech, and what remained of the building began sliding over the edge of the precipice. I wrapped my arms around a wall joist as an upright piano slid past me into the void.

I could hear the drunken revelers in the parking lot deliver another cheer as the last section of the building teetered over the edge. Glancing up at the sky for the last time, I saw something painted orange hovering about twenty feet above me. At first, the image didn't register clearly in my exhausted brain.

Then I saw it was the top end of a large crane, and I remembered the fire truck I had seen parked in the road next to the building. A man in some kind of harness was dangling below it.

He was descending in my direction when the front and side walls caved in and the building lost all form and shape. I watched him detach a coil of line from his tool belt and hurl it toward me. The end of the line reached my outstretched hands, and I gripped it with all my remaining strength.

The world went dark again for a moment as the walls came together. Then I found myself jerked upward through the wooden timbers. Head down, I saw the last of the Fall Creek Tavern disappear over the precipice in a long, tormented scream.

Thirty seconds later, my rescuer deposited me gently in the street next to the fire truck. As I touched ground, Kelly broke through the Groton police cordon and locked me in a tight embrace. Another loud cheer went up from the revelers.

"Baby," she cried, "how did you get way up there?"

29

The fireman who saved my life came lumbering toward me in his shiny orange outfit. As he got closer, I saw that it was a form-fitting suit made of fire-retardant fabric. The belt and pockets were studded with hooks and loops that contained his rescue gear. The brawny young man had a wild tangle of blond hair and a full beard to go with it.

"I owe you my life. Thanks," I said.

"When they told me it was Tank Cantrell, I asked to go up," he said, giving me a bear-toothed smile. "My father took me to see you play when I was twelve years old. I loved the way you ran over those linebackers. You weren't afraid of shit."

"Yeah, well . . . I'll buy you a barrel of beer one of these days."

"I'll drink it," he said, shaking my hand.

"Your eyes, honey," Kelly said, staring at me with genuine concern. "They have dried blood all around them. Let me nurse you, baby."

I could see Lauren Kenniston staring at us from next to the fire truck, and for some reason I felt embarrassed.

"I still have work to do," I said, gently breaking the clinch.

Captain Morgo was still talking into her radio when I limped around the side of the fire truck. Her police cruiser was parked right behind it. She signed off as I came up to her. Lauren joined us there.

"Welcome home," said Janet.

"He was up there . . . General Taylor," I said. "He shot himself when I tried to take him out with me. They'll find him in the wreckage at the bottom of the gorge."

"I sent Ken out to your cabin, Jake. Your dog is still alive."

"Thanks."

It was the best news I could have heard at that moment. Behind me, I could hear an ambulance racing up the steep grade from town. Its siren died to a groan as it pulled up next to her cruiser.

"Get in," ordered Captain Morgo.

I shook my head.

"There's one more thing I have to do. Will you drive me back to my pickup?"

"You're impossible," she growled before opening the passenger door for me.

"Can I talk to you later?" asked Lauren.

"Sure. I promised you an exclusive. Just leave me out of it."

"That won't be so easy," she said with a grin.

"Do your best."

Janet and I were on our way back to the campus security building when I asked, "What made you change your mind about me? It can't be just because I was right about Wheatley."

She glanced across the front seat.

"All I knew about your past was what Jim Dickey told me . . . that you had caused the deaths of your own men through negligence and cowardice. Jordan Langford told me the truth yesterday afternoon when I asked him about it . . . I'm sorry I didn't ask sooner, Jake."

"Life is pretty crazy," I said.

"Yeah," she agreed, "and tomorrow I'll be the bitch boss again."

I laughed.

"Get some rest," she called out to me as I got in the pickup.

The chance to close my eyes and know that someone wasn't trying to kill me. I was ready. And I wouldn't screw it up with bad dreams. But first I needed to see Jordan. I checked my watch. It was twenty minutes to five, the deadline he had set for himself to resign unless the blackmailer was stopped.

Wheatley's money, I kept thinking. It was what had led to his own murder when he decided to try to make amends for a fraternity prank gone wrong. Now his major financial gift to Jordan had led to blackmail.

Driving over to his house, I could feel the storm finally moving away on its path to the northeast. The wind was still gusting hard, but the sky was growing lighter by the minute.

Jordan's home overlooked the railroad tracks that cut through the poorest neighborhood in Groton. After being chosen as president of St. Andrews, he had informed his board of trustees that he didn't want to live in the president's house. He had told me it was Blair's idea. "I refuse to live in a mausoleum," she had said.

The house was modest, even by Groton standards, a 1940s colonial covered with asbestos shingles. A well-kept garden flanked the driveway onto the property, its flowers and plantings now crushed by the rain and wind. At the end of the driveway, I was surprised to see a red Ferrari parked behind Jordan's green Volvo. It had probably cost three times more than the house.

When I knocked on the kitchen door, it was opened by a short, plump man wearing a double-breasted gray worsted suit. He had thick pomaded hair, close-set eyes, and a broad face that broke into an ingratiating smile when he saw who it was.

I wasn't ingratiated. Even in my diminished mental state, it wasn't too hard to recognize him. His and his brother's faces graced the back cover of several hundred thousand telephone books in upstate New York. I wondered what Brian Razzano was doing there.

When he reached out to shake my hand, a Rolex Oyster emerged like a small turtle from within his white silk shirt sleeve. I ignored his hand, and he dropped it awkwardly to his side.

"I was hoping to get a chance to talk to you alone, Jake," he said. "Before you see Jordan, I mean."

When I pushed past him, he followed me down the hallway into their kitchen.

"Since you called me this morning, I've learned that it's remotely possible Bob Devane was potentially engaged in blackmailing some of my clients. If it's true, I want you to know that I knew nothing about it. I swear to you, Jake."

I stopped and turned around. He was gazing up at me as if receiving my personal blessing was his only goal in life.

"So you just used Devane to spy on behalf of your legitimate clients, is that it?"

"Every good criminal lawyer needs a reputable investigative firm. I was shocked to learn that Bob might possibly have abused my trust. Of course the jury is still out."

His gambler's eyes were waiting to see if I actually believed him. I had no way of knowing whether he was telling the truth or not. At that point, I was too exhausted to care.

"Where's Jordan?" I asked.

"He's in his study. Blair's waiting in the living room and was hoping she might see you first."

"You have it all choreographed, don't you? Where's the study?"

"Through there," he said, pointing to a door next to the kitchen.

It led down to the basement. Jordan's study turned out to be a cubicle along the back wall. To get to it, I had to duck under iron water pipes and metal ductwork, then squeeze past the oil burner and the hot water heater.

The back of the basement had been outfitted as an office for him and Blair, with two computer desks, two computer stations, and a double file cabinet. A black-and-white poster of Mohandas Gandhi was taped to the cheap paneling above the desks.

Jordan was wearing jeans and a flannel shirt as he typed on his keyboard and stared into the computer screen. From the back, he looked the way he did when we were students and he would hammer out a term paper on his portable Olivetti.

"Now I know where all your money goes," I said.

He turned to look up at me, his haggard face flashing a rueful grin.

"The truth is, we spend most of it as soon as my paycheck comes in."

"On what?" I asked. It certainly wasn't the current surroundings.

"On causes. We support a lot of causes . . . AIDS babies in Botswana, Habitat for Humanity, water projects in Bangladesh, inner-city schools—you name the cause, man, Blair is there with our checkbook to support it. I think she's trying to prove to Jesus that well-off people can fit through the eye of the needle."

"There are less noble ways to spend it," I said, thinking of the Ferrari in the driveway.

"Blair has never lost her devotion to good works. And she's never quite found the right niche here. She hates being the president's wife."

"Yeah . . . well, I'm not here for that."

"No."

I dropped wearily into the other plastic office chair.

"Need a drink?" he asked.

Lying, I shook my head no.

"Janet Morgo called a few minutes ago to say you solved the bridge murders."

I briefly told him what had happened since our last conversation. When I finished, I said, "I'm sorry, but it doesn't look like the two cases were connected after all, aside from the fact that Wheatley's money was at the root of both."

He grimaced.

"I guess I knew it wasn't really possible."

"I tried. I just ran out of time."

Taking in my physical condition, he said, "I hope you're not hurting too badly."

"I'm okay."

I didn't tell him that I had killed the man who had been filming him. That could wait.

"A few hours ago, I told Blair I was being blackmailed," he said. "I . . . told her it was something related to a trip I took to Cuba last year . . . something political."

"Did she buy it?"

"I don't know. She got very upset."

"Yeah . . ."

"Well . . . I need a few minutes to finish this resignation statement," he said, not turning away soon enough for me to see his eyes fill with tears.

I was retracing my steps past the oil burner when he called out, "Blair wants me to go back to Detroit again."

"You were good at it," I said.

"It's only now that I'm about to lose my damn job that I realize how much it matters to me. You don't know the kind of difference I could make here in the years ahead. Education on the world stage is changing so fast, Jake . . . oh, well . . . in another life."

"Yeah . . . the next one."

"Jake . . . Blair started drinking right after I told her about my being blackmailed. Could you try to reassure her that things will turn out all right?"

"Brian Razzano is up there doing that," I said, trying to keep the edge out of my voice.

"Yes . . . he and his wife, Dawn, have been here off and on since this morning. I might have told you that she and Blair have become good friends since he joined the board of trustees. Look, you've known both of us for a long time, Jake . . . just tell her this isn't the end of the world."

"Sure, Jordan," I said, trudging up the basement steps.

When I walked into the living room, Blair was sitting on the rattan couch with her long slender legs resting on the coffee table in front of it. She was dressed in a cotton blouse and tight-fitting stretch pants that accentuated the fine curves of her figure.

She was holding a tumbler of what looked like heavy cream with froth on top. A big Siamese cat was curled up on the couch next to her. Brian Razzano sat on the other side of the cat, trying to look thoughtful.

"Is Jordan still preparing his resignation speech?" she asked, slurring the words.

"Get out," I said to Razzano.

His thoughtful look disappeared. He didn't move.

"I told you to get out," I repeated.

She turned toward him and said, "S'allll right, Brian."

Razzano got up from the couch.

"I'll be right outside if you need anything, babe."

When he turned to leave, I saw that the back of his suit jacket and pants were covered with Siamese cat hair. For some reason, it temporarily improved my mood. I heard the back door close behind him, and it was quiet again.

"'Babe'?" I repeated sarcastically.

"He's in love with me," she said. "He and Dawn are having problems."

"I wonder why. When did Jordan first tell you he was going to resign?"

"Um . . . this afternoon," she said, sipping her drink.

I heard the low throaty growl of the Ferrari as Razzano started it up in the driveway.

"Did he tell you why?"

"I'm not sure if I'm supposed to tell you," she said. "Do you know?"

I shook my head.

"He said it was something that happened on the trip he made to Cuba last year," she said. "Some political thing."

She began studying me through red-rimmed eyes, her chin resting on her closed fist.

"The immortal Jake," she said, attempting to smile.

Her face collapsed, and tears began running silently down her cheeks.

"What are you drinking?" I asked, sitting down in one of the easy chairs facing her.

"It's Kahlua . . . and vodka, and . . . Bailey's Irish Cream . . . Brian mixes them for me. It's my third one. He says it's called a blow job."

She giggled through the tears.

"What a great guy," I said.

Her mind had already traveled elsewhere.

"We don't need any of this," she said. "We can go back to Detroit . . . it was so good there when we were starting out at ground zero . . . we can start the center again. It will be something good . . . something meaningful."

"He's already doing something meaningful."

"This shit?"

Part of the drink slopped over the edge of the glass.

"What are you so angry about?" I asked.

"Everything . . . this place . . . my role as his glorified robe fluffer . . . you name it," she said, taking a long sip of Razzano's drink. "This country is so pathetic right now . . . a culture that deifies excess without restraint, the degradation of women, sexual release without love or even caring, friends with all the benefits, celebrity without accomplishment, and the pure worship of money and greed," she said, the words smearing together, "while billions of people around the world wake up every day not knowing if they will even survive."

"Things haven't changed very much in three thousand years, have they?"

"Screw you, Jake," she said defiantly. "I still believe that Jordan and I can make a real difference . . . one person at a time."

Something gnawed at my muddled brain. I tried to remember what it might be.

"This tastes awful," she said, making a face after taking another swallow of her drink.

"Then don't drink it," I suggested, standing up to leave.

I was going through the kitchen when I heard a stifled sob coming up the basement stairs from the study. *Sorry, old buddy,* I silently apologized. Opening the back door, I headed outside.

Behind their old Volvo, I could see Razzano in his blood-red sports car. He had put on a red baseball cap embossed with the logo of the Ferrari racing team and was holding the steering wheel as if he was coming into the last straightaway at Monza.

"Friends with all the benefits," I said aloud.

Turning around, I went back inside the house. Blair was sitting exactly where I had left her. The Siamese cat had crawled onto her lap and was licking its paws contentedly. They looked up at the same time.

"Friends with all the benefits," I repeated.

"What?" she asked.

"In your little rant, you used the phrase 'friends with all the benefits.'"

"Friends with benefits is a very common term today," she came back. "I assume you know what it means."

"I know what it means," I said. "But you said friends with all the benefits. It's the name of a local call-girl service."

"I don't know what you're talking about," she said, continuing to stroke the cat.

"You told me you loathed being the president's wife. Remember?"

"In Detroit, we were full partners . . . we were making a real difference in people's lives. How would you like to be relegated to the role of the adoring wife whose sole contribution is to stand at the side of my perfect husband and bat my eyelashes up at him?"

The anger had focused her attention. It was finally starting to make sense.

"I probably should have figured it out before now," I said. "He's not so perfect, is he?"

"What are you talking about?" she asked while continuing to stroke the blue-eyed Siamese.

"I'm talking about your sending Jordan the video and giving him the demand for five million dollars from Wheatley's unrestricted gift. He told you about the gift, didn't he?"

"What video? You're not making any sense, Jake."

"That's why you came out to visit me at the lake, isn't it? Razzano wanted to know how much I had learned about the blackmail scheme."

She had run out of words.

"You and Razzano cooked this up together. You're fucking him, aren't you?"

"Why not?" she came right back. "At least he cares about me and what I think."

"Yeah. Five million dollars' worth."

"You're wrong about that. Instead of Jordan spending the money on another lame building, it would have gone to all the causes I believe in. Brian was setting up a foundation. I would have controlled it. Now that Jordan is resigning, it doesn't matter."

"Yeah, you would have controlled it. You don't know your new partner. Behind the curtain, he isn't the Wizard of Oz. Blackmail is his business. His idea of doing good is corrupting judges and politicians and buying more influence. And he was happy to add Jordan to the list."

"You're wrong about Brian."

"And you're a gullible fool. It ends now, Blair, or I'll turn you and Razzano over to the DA."

She started to cry again.

"How did you find out what he was doing?" I asked her softly.

Her eyes seemed infinitely sad.

"You think you know someone so well," she said. "On certain days, he just acted . . . so strangely. I knew something was going on. One night I borrowed a car and just followed him up to that place . . . you can't imagine . . . when I saw them through the opening in the curtains."

"Can you forgive him?" I asked.

"I don't know," she said, swallowing the last of her blow job.

"I can understand how you feel . . . the private humiliation of seeing him that way the first time. And then when you found out what he was doing, you asked counselor Brian for help . . . and he contracted the video job out after giving you some tender solace. And you convinced yourself that five million dollars could do a lot more good than the money in Jordan's paycheck. Except once you went down the blackmail road, Razzano would have taken most of it for himself."

She was staring hard at me now.

"You're going to go down there now and tell Jordan he can keep his job . . . that the blackmailer just called to let him off the hook. Tell him anything you want as long as you give him the miraculous reprieve."

She didn't say anything.

"He loves this job, Blair, and you need to let him keep it. Find something constructive to do with your time aside from fucking Razzano."

"All right," she said finally.

"And if you want to save your marriage, wait a few days and tell him the truth about what you did . . . and that he doesn't have to worry about being publicly exposed. Tell him that the master video file was destroyed. I have it, and I'll get rid of it."

She nodded as I tried to stand up. My body felt like dead weight as I walked back through the kitchen and out the back door.

Razzano was still sitting in his Ferrari while continuing to rev the twelve-cylinder engine. I could hear the repetitive beat of a rap song blaring from the car's sound system through the closed windows. I stopped at the driver's-side door. He pressed a switch on the center console, and the window rolled down.

"Anything I can do to help?" he asked earnestly over the pounding music.

"Yeah," I said, leaning into the car and pulling him toward me by his silk tie. "If you breathe a word to anyone about what Jordan did at the Wonderland, or if you continue trying to blackmail him, I'll kill you, Brian . . . just like your hard boy, Sal Scalise."

Letting him go, I began walking back to my truck. I couldn't tell if he believed me, but he turned down the rap music.

My battery was dead when I tried to start the engine. I wasn't about to ask Razzano for booster cables. Fortunately, Jordan lived on a hillside. Letting my foot off the brake, I let the truck roll back down the driveway and jumpstarted it.

Heading down Campus Hill, I was glad to know that Bug was still alive. I would find out from Ken Macready where she was and bring her home. I was ready to go home. I really missed home.

Acknowledgments

I would like to thank the gifted Kim Hastings for her contributions to this novel. And much appreciation to my editors at Crooked Lane, Matthew Martz and Peter Senftleben, whose recommendations made the book a more compelling and hopefully enjoyable read. And finally to my sainted literary agent, David Halpern, who has guided my writing career for eighteen years.